MW01590766

Chapter One

"I hate fireworks."

"I know, and you don't have to go. You can stay here at Hangman's House, and we'll do a silence spell. It should hold long enough for the fireworks display," I offered.

"You need me," Meri declared. "I cannot just let you go off galivanting all over town without me. What if there's trouble? Hmm? Then what will you do?"

"Meri, you ditch me all of the time. Literally, you just walk off to do goddess knows what. Sometimes you don't even say anything before you go." I rolled my eyes but kept my head turned so he wouldn't see it.

"I saw that."

"No, you didn't."

"Yes, I did."

"I mean, Meri, I do need you, but Thorn and I will be okay for a couple of hours at the lake. I promise you we won't get ourselves into any trouble. And, you know, Thorn is the sheriff and all."

"Thorn.is.the.sheriff…" Meri said in a mocking tone before licking his paw and casually cleaning his ear.

"You are in a mood today."

"I just don't understand why this fireworks thing is necessary, Kinsley. It's barbaric. It's bad for wildlife and… less sophisticated pets. I mean, I'm fine. I'm not scared or anything. I just hate them."

"Mhmmm." I felt a huge pang of sympathy for him. Meri really wasn't scared of anything, but for some reason, the impending fireworks display had him frazzled.

"And you did nothing about it."

"I did nothing about it?"

"You could have put a stop to it. That was your duty."

"Meri, I'm sorry you're upset about this, but you're being a tad dramatic."

"Whatever."

"Whatever…" I returned, but he was already walking off.

I was about to ask him if he wanted to help me make a potion to help the fireworks extra special, but given his opinion on the matter, I decided to do it myself. Since he wanted me to somehow find a way to prevent the fireworks, I didn't figure he'd want to help me make them bigger and more bombastic.

I was home alone, other than Meri, since Laney and Hekate were still at summer camp with Bonkers. Thorn was at work, and I'd taken a day off from working at Summoned Goods & Sundries and Craft Donuts.

"Now," I said to myself, but I kinda hoped Meri was listening. He was in the living room, after all, pretending that he was ignoring me. "What do I need to make a safe but really cool fire spell for fireworks?"

"A brain in that big head of yours," he called from the other room.

"I'm sorry, I didn't hear you."

Silence.

Most of my supplies were organized and stored in the basement, so I headed for the basement door. I flipped on the light at the top of the stairs and started down.

Once in the basement, I headed over to the shelves that contained the ingredients I'd need and began to peruse the jars stacked neatly in rows. Just past a couple of the shelving units was the wall where the entrance to the tunnels under Coventry had been bricked over.

Sometimes, I wished they were still open. It would have made getting around Coventry far more convenient. But from what I'd heard, there were potential nasty things dwelling in there. Nothing so bad that we had to, like, do anything about it, but enough that they stayed all bricked up.

"Did you get lost?"

I turned around and Meri was seated at the top of the basement steps. "I thought you weren't talking to me."

"Now you're the one being dramatic."

I checked the jars I'd grabbed and realized that I was missing an ingredient. I needed some powdered volcanic rock, except that I didn't have any to grind up.

"You wouldn't happen to know where I might have some volcanic rock or dust stashed around the house, would you?" I asked.

"Hey, yeah. I saw some in the... no. No, Kinsley. We don't have volcanic rock stashed somewhere in the house."

"Wow, you are in a mood," I said as I headed back up the stairs with the jars I did have. "But I know what will make you feel better."

"You've decided to use your pull in the community to get the fireworks show canceled?"

I shot him a look. "First of all, my pull in the community is nearly nonexistent thanks to me bringing a certain cat back from the dead."

"I knew I should have been talking to the real boss," Meri groused.

"You mean my mother."

"Brighton would get it done."

"Second of all," I said ignoring him, "this is a much better idea. I need to stop by Summoned Goods & Sundries to get some volcanic rock, so we'll swing by the Brew Station and grab a coffee… and some bacon."

"We have food at home."

"Meri."

"Fine."

"Good."

I slipped my shoes onto my feet on the way out the door, and Meri trotted along behind me as we made our way to my car. The drive down to the square was uneventful, which wasn't always a guarantee in Coventry.

Once we'd parked in one of the spaces surrounding the square, Meri and I crossed the street and went into Brew Station. I'd had to make that concession before we left. I promised Meri we'd go to the coffee shop first, so he'd stop sighing and dramatically ignoring me while he sat right next to me in the passenger seat.

"Kinsley!" Viv called out cheerfully as soon as we were through the front door. "And Meri too! Good to see you guys."

"She lives!" A voice at a table near the counter startled me, and I turned to see Dorian seated there with a huge mug of coffee and his laptop open.

"Dorian, Viv, hello."

I felt a pang of guilt when it came to Dorian. I hadn't been to see him in too long. We kept up with each other through texts, but we hadn't spent nearly enough time together lately.

"Do you mind if we sit with you?" I asked Dorian.

"I'm a little busy," he said and motioned toward his laptop. But then his face broke into a huge smile. "I'm kidding, darling. I'd be offended if you didn't."

"K. Let me get my coffee and some bacon for Meri."

With that, I stepped up to the counter where Viv waited patiently to make my order herself. Not everyone got special treatment from the owner but being good friends with Viv had its perks.

"Today I think I'll change it up a bit and have a dirty iced chai latte, please. And an order of bacon for my feline companion."

"Oh, something a little spicy. I like it," Viv said. "We don't get many orders for those, but they're one of my favorites too. Hang on a sec, and I'll get your order right up."

I stood and watched as Viv made the chai tea latte and then a shot of espresso to dump in. The espresso was what made it "dirty" and gave it an extra kick of caffeine. One of her employees put the order of bacon into the countertop oven, so that was ready at just about the same time as my drink.

"So, are you going to the fireworks tonight?" Viv asked as she passed my order across the counter to me.

"I am. In fact, that's why I'm out and about. I'm making a little something to add some extra oomph to the fireworks, and I need an ingredient from my shop. But I promised Meri that we'd stop by for bacon. Plus, I'm always up to see your gorgeous face."

"You're just using me for my coffee," Viv teased in return.

"I would never," I said in mock offense. "Are you going? Please tell me you're going."

7

"I am. And I'm not catering or working at the event in any way. I just get to go and have a good time."

"Oh, yay! We hardly ever get to spend any time together. Do you want to sit with me and Thorn tonight? Or do you have a date or something?" I asked and narrowed my eyes. It was unusual for Viv to not be working, and I wondered if there was more to it.

Like a man.

She laughed. "There's no date. I mean, unless you count Dorian over there, but I'm not his type," she said with a wink.

"Hey, you're everybody's type," Dorian protested from the table. "Like Kinsley said, you're gorgeous."

Viv blushed a little. "You guys are too much. But yes, Dorian and I had planned on meeting up with you guys there."

"Sounds like a plan."

"I've got some things to finish up if I'm going to take the entire night off," Vivian said with a chuckle. "I'll see you guys later."

"Later, hon," Dorian said, and I offered Viv a wave as she disappeared into the back of the coffee shop.

"Dorian," I began, stirring my dirty iced chai latte as I took a seat across from him. Meri hopped onto the chair next to me, his eyes fixated on the plate of bacon. "What's that you're working on?"

Dorian glanced up from his laptop. "Ah, Kinsley, always the curious one. I'm working on an investigative piece."

"Really?" I asked, intrigued. "What's it about?"

Dorian leaned back in his chair, taking a sip of his coffee before answering. "It's about a conspiracy theory I stumbled upon online. It's quite the rabbit hole."

"A conspiracy theory? Getting back to your journalism roots?"

"Yes," Dorian confirmed. "It's about this theory that the world's major coffee chains are involved in a secret pact to control the global coffee market. Sounds ridiculous, I know, but there's a surprising amount of people who believe it."

I took a sip of my latte, my mind whirling with possibilities. "That sounds... fascinating. And a little crazy."

Dorian chuckled. "That's the thing about conspiracy theories. They're often a mix of the absurd and the plausible. That's what makes them so captivating."

Meri, who had been quietly munching on his bacon, suddenly looked up. "Are you going to mention the Brew Station in your article?"

Dorian shook his head. "No, Meri. This theory is about the big multinational chains. The Brew Station is safe from these wild speculations."

I nodded, intrigued. "That's good to hear. But still, be careful, Dorian. Conspiracy theories can lead you down some strange paths. I remember the last time you got involved with something like this," I said, my tone more serious than I intended.

Dorian looked at me, a smirk tugging at the corner of his mouth. "You're referring to the satanic church debacle?"

I cleared my throat, uncomfortable with the memory. "That, and the... werewolf thing. And I don't know if I'd brush it off as a debacle. It's your life."

I was concerned that Dorian might be upset that I was dredging up that particular past, but instead, he just chuckled. "Kinsley, I've learned from those experiences," he said, his laughter subsiding. "I assure you, there's no risk of me morphing into some malevolent creature while investigating a global coffee cartel."

I managed a small smile. "Good. I don't think I'm equipped to deal with any more friends-turning-into-beasts incidents. So, can I see what you're working on? I'm fascinated by the idea of a coffee cartel."

Just as Dorian was about to pull up a document on his laptop, a document that promised to reveal the intriguing findings of his latest research, the calm atmosphere of the Brew Station was abruptly shattered. The entrance door swung open with a force that suggested a whirlwind had just decided to make its presence known. Two women marched in, their voices echoing with intensity and determination that instantly commanded the attention of everyone present.

They started distributing flyers, their impassioned speeches about the adverse effects of fireworks on veterans, pets, and wildlife resonating through the café. "Fireworks may seem like harmless fun, but they're not!" one of them was saying. "They cause distress to veterans, terrorize pets, and disrupt local wildlife."

Their cause was clearly close to their hearts, and their fervor was infectious. One of the women was a familiar face. Her name was Linda, a well-known figure in town, albeit not a part of our magical community. She was an ordinary citizen, but her passion for activism was anything but ordinary. I wished I could reassure her, let her know about the spell I had decided to cast on the fireworks to prevent any harm or fear they might cause. But that was a secret I had to keep to myself.

As Linda enthusiastically voiced her concerns, she made a bold accusation. "These organizers are nothing less than terrorists," she declared, her voice ringing out in the café. "They should be held accountable for the destruction and distress caused by their barbaric entertainment."

Her words were a harsh indictment, causing a wave of unease to sweep through the café. Viv, always the peacemaker, swiftly stepped in. She approached the women with a calm and composed demeanor, her voice steady as she requested them to leave. "Ladies, I understand your concerns," she said, her tone soothing. "But this is a place of business. If you don't leave quietly, I'll have to call the sheriff."

In an attempt to defuse the escalating situation, Viv extended an olive branch. "Why don't you both have a coffee on the house?" she suggested, her gesture towards the counter accompanied by a warm smile.

The women seemed momentarily disarmed by the offer, their fiery protest briefly quelled. Linda looked at Viv, her anger giving way to surprise. "Well... all right," she said, her voice softer now. "But we won't stop fighting."

Viv looked at Linda and her friend, her expression calm and understanding. "You're more than welcome to fight for what you believe in," she said, her voice steady. "But I'd appreciate it if you could continue your campaign outside."

Linda and her friend exchanged glances, their expressions softening. "All right," Linda conceded. "But before we go, we'll take you up on that coffee offer."

The women ordered their drinks, opting for the most expensive, fancy coffee concoctions on the menu. Viv, however, didn't bat an eye. She set about making their drinks with the same care and attention she gave to every order. As she worked, she added, "And how about a pastry to go with your coffees? On the house."

The women seemed taken aback by Viv's generosity, but they accepted the offer. Once their orders were ready, they thanked Viv and left the café, their departure much quieter than their entrance.

With the women gone, Viv made her way over to our table. "Well, that was interesting," she said, a wry smile on her face.

"You handled that very generously, Viv," I said, impressed by her calm and tactful handling of the situation.

Viv shrugged, her smile widening. "It's always better to have friends than enemies, Kinsley. Even if those friends are passionate activists with a penchant for dramatic entrances."

Chapter Two

After finishing our drinks, Meri and I left the Brew Station and began our walk across the town square towards Summoned Goods & Sundries. The square was bustling with activity, a typical day in Coventry. But amidst the usual hustle and bustle, I spotted Linda and her friend, still fervently handing out their flyers.

I subtly adjusted our path, steering clear of the two activists. Meri, however, seemed to have other ideas. "You know, Kinsley," he began, his voice filled with a rare seriousness, "I agree with Linda and her friend. You should stop the fireworks display."

I sighed, glancing down at Meri. "Don't worry, Meri, I'm going to put extra magic in the spell I'm working on. It'll make it so the fireworks don't bother anyone who isn't into them. That includes you, my friend. You won't even hear them with this spell… no silence shroud over Hangman's House needed."

Meri let out a laugh, a sound that was more of a snort. "Given your track record with magic, Kinsley, you'll probably end up blowing Coventry right off the map."

I rolled my eyes at his comment but couldn't suppress a smile. "Thanks for the vote of confidence, Meri."

As we continued our walk to the shop, I couldn't help but think about Meri's words. I knew my magic could be unpredictable at times, but I was determined to make this work. For the sake of Coventry, and for the sake of my feline friend, I had to ensure the fireworks display went off without a hitch.

Meri and I stepped into Summoned Goods & Sundries, and we were greeted by a sight that was both fascinating and alarming. A crystal ball, typically a stationary object, was in the process of morphing into a teapot. As I watched, a feather quill on the counter began to twist and contort, transforming into a spoon. Nearby, a candlestick reshaped itself into a flower vase.

"Meri," I said, my voice barely above a whisper, "are you seeing this?"

Meri, who had been sniffing at a corner, looked up. "The shapeshifting objects? Yeah, I see them. Weird."

Before I could respond, the stockroom door creaked open, and my manager, Reggie, appeared.

"Kinsley," she said, her voice laced with relief. "I'm glad you're here. This situation is escalating, and I'm at a loss."

I gestured at the shapeshifting objects, my eyebrows furrowed. "You mean this? Any idea what's causing it?"

Reggie shook her head. "I'm clueless. It started about an hour ago. So far, the tourist customers haven't noticed anything. They seem to think it's part of the shop's 'magical' charm. But we need to figure out what's happening and fix it before it becomes too noticeable or spirals out of control."

I nodded, my mind whirring with possibilities. This was far from a typical day at Summoned Goods & Sundries.

Together, Reggie and I began to scour the shop, searching for any clues that might explain the strange phenomenon. After a few minutes, Reggie called out from a corner of the shop.

"Kinsley, I've found something!" she said, holding up a parchment. It was inscribed with a spell, but I didn't recognize the magic inscribed on it. Well, not exactly anyway... it wasn't witchcraft.

"Let's take this to my office," I suggested. "We can review the security footage and try to identify who left this."

Reggie and I made our way to my office. I sank into my chair, the familiar creak of the leather a welcome sound amidst the day's strangeness. Reggie pulled up a chair next to me, her eyes focused and alert.

I brought up the shop's security footage on the screen, rewinding to the time when the shapeshifting objects had first started. Together, we scrutinized every frame, every movement, searching for any sign of what could have triggered the phenomenon.

Finally, we saw her. A woman with hair so black it shimmered with an almost sapphire-blue hue under the shop's lights. Even through the video footage, I could sense a strange energy radiating from her, a power that was both intriguing and unsettling.

As she turned to face the camera, a chill ran down my spine. Her face was eerily familiar. For a moment, she looked like me. Then, her features shifted, and she bore an uncanny resemblance to my mother. And then, just as quickly, she turned away from the camera.

"Whoa," Reggie breathed out, her eyes wide. "Did you see that?"

I nodded, my mind reeling. "Shapeshifting tricksters," I mumbled, a note of frustration creeping into my voice. "I'm getting tired of them."

Reggie turned to me, her expression serious. "What should we do, Kinsley?"

I thought for a moment, then said, "We should burn the parchment."

Reggie looked taken aback. "Is that safe?"

"I think so," I replied. "I believe this whole thing is just a message for me. It should be safe."

With that, Reggie, Meri, and I headed out into the alley behind the shop. I held the parchment in my hand, its strange script seeming to shimmer in the light. With a deep breath, I set it alight. The parchment burned quickly, leaving nothing but ashes.

When we returned to the shop, it was as if nothing had happened. The objects had returned to their normal states, no longer shifting and changing. The shop was back to its usual self, the earlier chaos nothing more than a memory. But the image of the woman with the sapphire-blue hair lingered in my mind. I had an idea of who "she" was, and that notion ticked me right the heck off.

But, with the peculiar shapeshifting incident behind us, I finally had the opportunity to retrieve the volcanic rock I needed for my spell. I navigated my way to the elemental stores, a corner of the shop dedicated to natural elements, and picked out a suitable piece of volcanic rock.

Carrying it downstairs, I fetched a mortar and pestle from one of the shelves. I could have easily done this at home, but just as I was about to start grinding the rock into a fine powder, the front door chimed, announcing a new arrival.

Azura, one of my employees, sauntered in, her belly round with pregnancy. It looked as if she was smuggling a watermelon under her shirt, but her face was alight with a radiant smile.

"Hey, Azura," I greeted her, setting the mortar and pestle on the counter. "You're absolutely glowing! How's the little one treating you?"

Azura placed a hand on her belly, her smile widening. "We're both doing great, Kinsley. Sol and I are over the moon. We can't wait to welcome our baby."

"That's fantastic, Azura," I replied, resuming my task of grinding the rock. "Keeping the gender a surprise, right?"

She nodded, her eyes sparkling with anticipation. "Yes, we thought it would add to the magic of the moment when we finally meet them."

I chuckled. "That's a beautiful idea, Azura. You're going to be a wonderful mother."

Azura blushed slightly, her hand instinctively rubbing her belly. "Thank you, Kinsley. That means a lot." As I continued grinding the volcanic rock into a fine powder, Azura brought up a new topic. "Kinsley, I was thinking about decorating the shop and the storefront for the festival. With all the tourists in town for the festivities and the fireworks show, it might attract more customers."

I looked up from my task, considering her suggestion. "That sounds like a fantastic idea, Azura. Just remember not to overdo it. We don't want to scare away our regulars with too much glitz."

Azura chuckled. "Don't worry, Kinsley. Sol is coming in a bit to help, and we'll keep it tasteful. Reggie told me to clear it with you before we started putting anything up."

I nodded, pleased with their initiative. "That's great, Azura. I trust your judgment. Go ahead with the decorations."

With the decision made to decorate the shop for the festival, I decided to stay on and see what creative magic Azura and Sol would weave. However, I still had my own task to complete… the potion. Gathering my ingredients, including the freshly ground volcanic rock, I retreated to the privacy of my office.

Once inside, I spread out my ingredients on the large wooden desk. The potion I was about to create was a complex one, designed to both enhance the fireworks display and silence the noise for those who wished to avoid it. It was a delicate balance, requiring precise measurements and careful blending of the ingredients.

As I worked, the rhythmic motion of stirring and the soft whisper of the ingredients mixing together created a soothing cadence. The process of potion-making was always a meditative one for me, allowing my mind to focus on the task at hand while also letting it wander and dream.

Meri, ever the "curious" observer, jumped onto the desk, his eyes following my every move. "So, you're really going to try to pull this off, huh?" he said, his tone laced with his usual snark.

"Yes, Meri, and your commentary is not helping," I retorted, shooting him a playful glare.

He flicked his tail, a smirk playing on his feline features. Undeterred, Meri continued his commentary. "Just remember, Kinsley, if you blow up the town, I'm blaming you."

I chuckled at his dramatic statement, shaking my head as I continued to stir the potion. "Noted, Meri. I'll make sure to keep that in mind."

As I worked, Meri continued to watch, his commentary a constant background noise. His remarks, though sometimes exasperating, were a part of the process.

Once the potion was complete, I carefully poured it into a small vial, corking it securely. Wrapping it in a protective cloth, I placed it safely in my bag. "All right, Meri," I said. "Let's go see what Azura and Sol have done with the place."

Meri hopped off the desk, following me as I made my way downstairs. As we emerged from the office, we were greeted by a dazzling display of decorations. Azura and Sol had truly outdone themselves.

Inside, the shop was a riot of red, white, and blue. Streamers hung from the ceiling, twisting and turning in the air currents, their shiny surfaces catching the light and casting colorful reflections around the room. Small flags adorned the shelves, nestled between the various magical items. Even the counter was decked out, a tablecloth with a star-spangled pattern draped over it.

Outside, the storefront was equally festive. A banner proclaiming 'Happy 4th of July!' stretched across the top, its bold letters standing out against the bright blue background. Red, white, and blue balloons bobbed in the breeze, tied to the door handle and the signpost. The windows were adorned with decals of fireworks, their vibrant colors promising a spectacular show.

After taking a moment to admire their handiwork, I left the shop, Meri trailing behind me. Our next stop was the library, where I was to deliver the potion to Isadora, the fire witch who would be heading the fireworks show that evening.

Isadora worked in the magic wing of the library, a section filled with ancient tomes and magical artifacts.

I found her sorting through a pile of books, her fiery red hair tied back in a loose bun.

"Isadora," I greeted her, holding out the vial. "I've got the potion for tonight's show."

She looked up, her eyes lighting up as she took the vial from me. "Thank you, Kinsley," she said, her voice filled with gratitude. "This will make tonight's show truly spectacular."

As I handed over the potion, I couldn't help but notice that Isadora seemed a bit frazzled. Her usually neat bun was slightly askew, and there was a certain tension in her shoulders.

"Everything okay, Isadora?" I asked, concern creeping into my voice.

She glanced up at me, her eyes momentarily reflecting the stress she was under. But then she smiled, a small but genuine smile, and nodded. "Yes, everything's fine, Kinsley. Just a bit overwhelmed with the preparations for tonight's show."

I nodded in understanding. Organizing a fireworks display, especially a magical one, was no small feat. "I'm sure it's going to be amazing," I reassured her.

We then moved on to discussing the details of the fireworks display. Isadora shared her plans, her eyes lighting up as she described the different magical fireworks she had prepared. It was clear that despite the stress, she was passionate about her work.

As we chatted, Isadora suddenly asked, "How are Laney and Hekate enjoying their time at summer camp?"

I smiled at the mention of my daughters. "They're having a blast," I replied. "They've been sending me pictures and updates. It seems like they're making the most of their summer adventure."

Isadora smiled, her eyes softening. "That's wonderful to hear. They deserve a fun and carefree summer."

"They do. Well, I better be going. I'll see you tonight at the show."

As Meri and I were making our way out of the library, the front doors swung open with a bang. Mayor Miles Taylor stormed in, his face set in a grimace. He brushed past me without a word of greeting, his focus solely on Isadora, who was crossing the lobby from the magical wing into the mundane wing of the library.

His sudden appearance and the tension radiating off him piqued my curiosity. I slowed my pace, pretending to adjust the strap of my bag while I tried to catch snippets of their conversation.

Mayor Taylor was speaking in a hushed but heated tone, his words echoing in the quiet library. "Isadora, this library's budget is getting out of hand. We can't keep pouring funds into it without seeing some return."

Isadora, taken aback by his abruptness, tried to reason with him. "Mayor Taylor, the library is not a business. It's a public service. Its value can't be measured in dollars and cents."

I could see the mayor's face turning a shade redder at her words. He opened his mouth to retort when his gaze landed on me. His eyes narrowed, and he shot me a pointed glare, clearly indicating that I was intruding.

Taking the hint, I quickly made my way out of the library, Meri trotting along beside me. As the library doors closed behind me, I couldn't help but wonder what the outcome of that conversation would be.

Chapter Three

"Meri, can we talk about why you hate fireworks so much?"

I was standing at the kitchen counter kneading a huge ball of dough. I'd needed something to keep my hands busy, so I decided to make bread. It made sense to me.

"No," Meri groused from his perch on a nearby stool, his tail flicking in annoyance.

"Oh, come on. There's got to be a story there," I prodded, glancing over at him. His eyes were narrowed, a clear sign of his irritation.

"It would be different if you were making bacon instead of bread. I'm not a fan," he retorted, his gaze lingering on the dough as if it had personally offended him.

I chuckled at his comment, shaking my head. "You can't live on bacon alone, Meri."

"Watch me," he shot back, a hint of his usual snark returning.

I chuckled at his comment, shaking my head slightly. "Besides, homemade bread is delicious."

As I continued to knead the dough, my mind wandered back to the stories I'd heard about Meri. He was once a powerful witch who'd somehow landed in hot water with his coven. As a result, he'd been transformed into a cat, destined to serve my family's line for eternity.

A thought struck me then, a connection I hadn't considered before. Could his aversion to fireworks have something to do with his past transgression? The one that led to his transformation?

"Meri," I began, my voice soft but steady. "Does your dislike for fireworks have anything to do with... well, with what happened? With why you were turned into a familiar?"

Meri's eyes widened slightly, and he let out a dramatic sigh. "Oh, here we go," he grumbled, rolling his eyes. "Kinsley's playing detective again."

I couldn't help but chuckle at his response. "I'm just curious, Meri."

"Well, maybe I'm just a cat who hates loud noises," he retorted, his tail flicking in annoyance. "Ever think of that, Sherlock?"

His snarky response brought a smile to my face. "All right, all right," I conceded, raising my hands in surrender. "I'll drop it."

"Good," he huffed, settling back down on the stool. "Now, can we get back to the important matter at hand? Like when that bread will be ready?"

Despite his prickly response, I couldn't help but feel that there was more to it. But for now, I decided to let the matter rest. After all, Meri was entitled to his secrets, just like the rest of us.
"I was thinking about using this bread to make sandwiches for a picnic at the lake later during the fireworks display," I mused aloud, glancing at Meri. "Turkey and Swiss, maybe. But I think they'd be even better with some bacon."

At the mention of bacon, Meri's ears perked up. He tried to maintain his nonchalant facade, but I could see the interest in his eyes. "Whatever," he said, attempting to sound indifferent. But he didn't move from his spot on the stool, his gaze fixed on me.

I chuckled, turning to the fridge to pull out the bacon. "I'll make some extra for you," I promised, placing the bacon in the frying pan. The sizzle and aroma filled the kitchen, and I could see Meri's tail twitching in anticipation.

As I cooked, Meri settled down on the stool, his eyes never leaving the pan. Despite his earlier grumbling, it was clear that he was looking forward to the bacon.

As I was finishing up assembling the sandwiches and packing them up for the picnic, a sudden knock at the front door startled me. Wiping my hands on a kitchen towel, I walked over to the door and swung it open.

Standing on the porch was Isadora, her face pale and her eyes wide with fear. "Isadora?" I greeted, taken aback by her appearance. "What's wrong?"

But before she could answer, her mouth opened in what looked like a silent scream. My heart pounded in my chest as she suddenly burst into flames. Instinctively, I reached for my magic, trying to douse the fire engulfing her.

But as I cast my spell, Isadora disappeared in a puff of smoke. The porch was suddenly empty, the only evidence of her presence the lingering smell of smoke.

"Meri!" I called out, my voice shaky. "Meri, something's happened to Isadora!"

"What?" came Meri's nonchalant reply from the kitchen. Confused, I turned around and found myself back in the kitchen, a bagged sandwich in my hand. The front door was closed, and there was no sign of Isadora or the fire.

I blinked, my mind struggling to make sense of what had just happened. Had it all been a hallucination? But it had felt so real...

"Meri," I began, my voice shaky, "I just had the strangest hallucination. Isadora was at the door, and then she... she burst into flames."

Meri's ears perked up at this, his gold eyes meeting mine. "That sounds like a psychic premonition," he said, his tone serious.

"But visions aren't really my thing," I protested, my mind still reeling from the vivid hallucination. "I mean, I've always had good intuition, but this..."

Meri flicked his tail, his gaze never leaving mine. "You should find a way to call off the fireworks," he suggested.

I sighed, running a hand through my hair. "Meri, I don't know how I could possibly do that so close to the show."

He shrugged, a nonchalant gesture that seemed out of place given the situation. "Tell Isadora that if she goes through with them, she's going to die."

I blinked at him, taken aback by his suggestion. "That's... that's too dramatic, Meri. I don't even know if it's a premonition."

Meri simply stared at me, his gaze steady. "Then find out."

And that's when it hit me. Adi. Adi at The Psychic Experience could help. She was the town's resident psychic, and if anyone could help me figure out what was going on, it was her.

"All right," I said, determination settling in. "I'm going to go see Adi. Maybe she can help."

With that, I grabbed my bag and headed for the door, Meri trailing behind me. Whatever was going on, I was going to get to the bottom of it.

When I arrived at The Psychic Experience, Adi was just finishing up with a client. I waited patiently as she exchanged pleasantries with the client, a woman who looked relieved and grateful as she paid Adi and left the shop.

Once the door had closed behind her, Adi turned to me, her brow furrowed in concern. "Kinsley, are you okay?" she asked, her voice filled with genuine concern.

"I need to talk," I admitted, my voice barely above a whisper.

Adi nodded, gesturing towards the back of the shop. "Come, sit. Would you like some tea? Or a Coke?"

I opted for the Coke, the familiar taste a small comfort in the face of the unknown. We settled down at her table, the crystal ball sitting innocuously in the center.

"Now, tell me what's wrong," Adi said, her gaze steady on mine.

I took a deep breath, the cool fizz of the Coke grounding me as I prepared to recount the vision. "Adi," I began, my voice steady despite the turmoil inside me, "I had a vision... or a hallucination, I'm not sure."

Adi's eyes widened slightly, but she remained silent, encouraging me to continue.

"It was Isadora," I continued, my grip tightening around the soda can. "She was at my door, and then... she was on fire, Adi. She was screaming, but no sound came out. And then she just... vanished. Turned into smoke."

The words tumbled out of me, a rush of fear and confusion. Adi listened, her gaze never leaving mine, her expression serious and thoughtful.

"And the strangest part," I added, my voice dropping to a whisper, "was that it felt so real. But then I was back in my kitchen, like nothing had happened."

Adi was silent for a moment, her gaze distant as she processed my words. "Kinsley," she finally said, her voice soft, "visions can be tricky. They can be symbolic, literal, or even a mix of both. But one thing is certain, they're never random. There's a reason you saw what you did."

"Thank you, Adi," I said, rising from the table. "I appreciate your insight."

Adi gave me a warm smile, her hand reaching out to give mine a reassuring squeeze. "Anytime, Kinsley. And remember, trust your instincts. They're usually right."

With a nod, I turned to leave, Meri jumping off the table to follow me. "Goodbye, Adi," I called over my shoulder, and she waved us off with a smile.

Once outside, Meri and I made our way to the library. The vision of Isadora was still fresh in my mind, and I knew I had to talk to her. I had to convince her to cancel the fireworks show. But when I found her in the library, engrossed in her work, and told her about my vision, she simply shook her head.

"Kinsley, everything will be fine," she assured me, her voice steady.

"But, Isadora, you don't understand. I saw you--" I began, but she cut me off.

"I can't afford to listen to your vision, Kinsley," she said, her voice firm. "The mayor is already upset with me. I can't risk the library budget."

I felt a pang of frustration, but I kept my voice calm. "You don't have to worry about that. My coven will make sure the mayor doesn't affect the library."

She seemed to consider this, her gaze thoughtful. "I appreciate that, Kinsley. But I'm a strong witch too. I can handle myself."

I didn't want to argue with her, so I simply nodded and left. My next stop was the mayor's office, but when I arrived, his secretary informed me that he wouldn't see me. I was left frustrated and worried, unsure of what to do next.

Feeling a sense of desperation creeping in, I pulled out my phone and dialed Thorn's number. He picked up after a couple of rings.

"Thorn," I began, my voice shaking slightly, "I need to tell you something. I had a vision... or a hallucination, I'm not sure."

There was a pause on the other end of the line, and I could almost hear him processing my words. "What kind of vision?" he asked, his voice filled with concern.

"It was Isadora," I continued, my grip tightening around the phone. "She was at my door, and then... she was on fire, Thorn. She was screaming, but no sound came out. And then she just... vanished. Turned into smoke."

I could hear Thorn's sharp intake of breath on the other end of the line. "Kinsley, that sounds serious," he said, his voice grave. "Is there anything you can do to stop the fireworks show?"

I could hear the worry in his voice, and it mirrored my own. "I tried talking to Isadora, but she won't listen. She says she can't risk the library budget. And the mayor won't see me. I don't know what to do, Thorn."

There was a pause on the other end of the line, and I could almost hear him thinking it over. "Kinsley, the town has all of the proper permits, and the show has been cleared by the fire department," he finally said, his voice filled with regret. "I'm sorry, but I can't stop it either."

His words felt like a punch to the gut, but I forced myself to keep my voice steady. "Darn, I'll have to figure out something else."

"Maybe we shouldn't go," he suggested, but I quickly dismissed the idea.

"No, I have to go," I said firmly. "I can't just turn my back on this."

There was another pause, and then Thorn sighed. "All right, Kinsley. I trust your judgment. I'll see you when I get off work."

"Wait, Thorn," I said before he could hang up. "I'm going to call my mom. Maybe she can help."

"Good idea," he agreed, and with that, we ended the call. I was left staring at my phone, my mind racing with worry and uncertainty.

With a deep breath, I dialed my mom's number. She picked up on the second ring.

"Mom," I began, my voice shaking slightly, "I need to talk to you about something."

I quickly explained the situation, my words tumbling out in a rush. When I finished, there was a moment of silence before my mom spoke.

"Kinsley," she said, her voice soothing, "with us there, the Aunties there, and the whole town watching, everything will be okay."

"But, Mom, I saw--"

"I know what you saw, sweetheart," she interrupted gently. "But you're probably just stressed because Meri is giving you a hard time about the fireworks. You know how relentless he can be."

I blinked in surprise. "How did you know about that?"

She laughed softly. "Kinsley, Meri was my familiar first. I know him better than anyone. Plus, he's been over to my house twice to complain about the fireworks."

I couldn't help but laugh at that. Trust Meri to go to such lengths. With my mom's reassurances, I felt a little better. Maybe everything would be okay after all.

Chapter Four

As the sun began to set, the Fourth of July celebrations in Coventry were in full swing. The town square was abuzz with excitement, the annual fireworks display being the highlight of the day. Families and friends gathered on blankets and lawn chairs, their faces lit up with anticipation.

Thorn, Meri, and I had claimed a spot on the grassy hill overlooking the lake, our blanket spread out beneath us. Viv and Dorian had joined us, their laughter mingling with the hum of the crowd. We sat there, munching on the sandwiches I had made earlier and sipping on homemade strawberry lemonade, the sweet-tart flavor a perfect complement to the warm summer evening.

As the sky darkened, the crowd grew quiet, their eyes fixed on the horizon. The first firework shot up into the sky, a bright streak of light that exploded into a shower of sparkling colors. A collective gasp went up from the crowd, followed by cheers and applause.

Despite the vision I had earlier, I couldn't help but get caught up in the magic of the moment. The fireworks lit up the night sky, their brilliant colors reflected in the lake below. It was a sight to behold, and for a moment, I allowed myself to forget my worries and simply enjoy the spectacle.

Meri, however, was less impressed. He sat on the blanket next to me, his ears flattened against his head and a disgruntled look on his face. But even he couldn't dampen the joy of the moment. As the fireworks continued to light up the night sky, I felt a sense of peace settle over me. Maybe my mom was right. Maybe everything would be okay after all...

Just as I was beginning to relax into the rhythm of the fireworks, a piercing scream cut through the night. The crowd fell silent, the festive atmosphere evaporating instantly. My heart pounded in my chest as I scanned the crowd, trying to locate the source of the scream.

Before I could pinpoint it, a loud explosion echoed through the air, much louder and closer than any of the fireworks. The crowd erupted into chaos, people scrambling to their feet and running in all directions. I felt a chill run down my spine as I turned towards the sound, my eyes widening in horror.

"Isadora!" I gasped, my mind flashing back to the vision I had earlier. I looked at Thorn, his face pale in the firelight. Without a word, we both got up and started running towards the lake, Meri hot on our heels. The sound of the crowd faded into the background as we raced towards the burning area, praying that we weren't too late.

Meri and I somehow managed to make it to the edge of the lake ahead of Thorn. The sight that met us was horrifying. Isadora was lying on the ground, her body badly burned and unconscious. The smell of burnt fabric and singed hair filled the air, making my stomach churn.

I dropped to my knees beside her, my hands shaking as I reached out to touch her. I could feel her life force, weak and flickering like a candle in the wind. I closed my eyes and focused, channeling my magic into her in an attempt to keep her alive.

But it was like trying to hold back a tidal wave with a sieve. I could feel her slipping away, her life force dwindling with every passing second. I gritted my teeth, pouring more of my magic into her, but it was like pouring water into a sieve. I just wasn't strong enough to heal her.

"Kinsley!" Thorn's voice echoed in my ears as he arrived, his footsteps pounding on the ground. "What happened?"

I didn't have the strength to answer. All I could do was keep pouring my magic into Isadora, praying that it would be enough to keep her alive until help arrived. But deep down, I feared it was a losing battle. I just wasn't strong enough.

Thorn was at my side in an instant, his phone already in his hand. "I'm calling for medical assistance," he said, his voice steady despite the chaos around us. I could hear him speaking urgently into the phone, giving our location and describing the situation.

Meanwhile, I tried to focus on Isadora. I could feel her life force, weak and flickering, but still there. I pushed my magic into her, trying to stabilize her, to keep her with us until help arrived.

As I worked, I tried to piece together what had happened. The explosion, the fire... it all pointed to a mishap with the fireworks. But was it an accident? Or was it something more sinister? My mind flashed back to the vision I had earlier, the vision of Isadora bursting into flames. Could it have been a premonition after all?

I shook my head, trying to clear my thoughts. Now was not the time for speculation. Right now, I needed to focus on Isadora, to keep her alive. The rest could wait until later.

As the sound of sirens grew louder in the distance, I took a deep breath and redoubled my efforts, pouring all of my magic into Isadora. I could only hope that help would arrive in time.

As I continued to channel my magic into Isadora, my hand brushed against her clothes. A strange sensation tingled at my fingertips, drawing my attention. I glanced down and my breath hitched.

There, on Isadora's clothes, was a faint shimmering residue. It was a sickening yellow color, like bile, pulsing with an eerie energy. It was faint, almost invisible, but unmistakable to someone who knew what to look for. It was the residue of a powerful spell.

A chill ran down my spine. This wasn't an accident. Someone had targeted Isadora with a spell. A powerful, destructive spell. I almost missed it because I was so focused on keeping her alive, but now that I had noticed it, I couldn't ignore it.

"Thorn," I called, my voice barely more than a whisper. He turned to look at me, his face etched with worry. "There's something you need to know."

As the paramedics arrived and began to work on Isadora, I quietly explained to Thorn about the magical residue. His eyes widened in shock, but he nodded, understanding the gravity of the situation. He wouldn't be able to see the residue or understand it as I did, but he trusted my judgment.

As I watched the paramedics load Isadora into the ambulance, a feeling of dread settled in my stomach.

This wasn't an accident. It was an attack. And I had a feeling that things were about to get a lot more complicated.

Once the ambulance had disappeared into the distance, Thorn and I turned our attention to the small group of people who had remained at the scene. The explosion had sent most of the crowd running, but a handful of people had stayed behind, their faces pale and shocked in the aftermath of the incident.

Thorn and I decided to split up to cover more ground. I approached a small group of people huddled together, their faces etched with worry and fear. I took a deep breath, steeling myself for the difficult conversations ahead.

"Excuse me," I began, my voice steady despite the turmoil inside me. "I know this is a difficult time, but I need to ask you a few questions about what happened."

The group turned to me, their eyes wide with shock and confusion. One woman, her eyes red and teary, nodded for me to continue.

"Did any of you see anything unusual before the explosion?" I asked.

A man in the group, his face ashen, spoke up. "There was a young woman arguing with Isadora before the show started."

"Do you know who she was?" I asked, my heart pounding in my chest.

The man nodded. "Her name's Belinda. She's a fire witch, like Isadora. She was supposed to be helping with the fireworks."

"Can you tell me more about their argument?" I pressed.

The man shook his head. "I couldn't hear what they were saying. But Belinda was shouting, and Isadora looked upset."

I thanked the man for his help and moved on to another group of witnesses. They echoed the man's account, adding that Belinda had seemed angry and frustrated. One woman even mentioned that she had seen Belinda storm off just before the fireworks started.

Armed with this new information, I quickly found Thorn and relayed what I had learned. His eyes narrowed at the mention of Belinda.

"We need to find her," he said, his voice firm. "She might know more about what happened. Oh, and I spoke with the emergency department," he said, his voice low. "Isadora is still in critical condition. Her injuries are extensive."

As Thorn relayed the grim news about Isadora's condition, a sense of urgency settled over us. We needed to find Belinda, and fast. We began to canvas the area, asking anyone who remained if they had seen a young woman with fiery hair and a fiery temper to match.

Most shook their heads, their faces a mix of confusion and concern. But one elderly man, his face lined with age and his eyes sharp, pointed us towards the lake. "Saw a lass fitting that description heading that way," he said, his voice gruff. "Looked upset, she did."

With a nod of thanks, we headed in the direction he had indicated. The area near the lake was quieter, the chaos of the explosion fading into a distant hum. We moved through the trees, our eyes scanning the shadows for any sign of Belinda.

Finally, we spotted her. She was hidden behind a cluster of bushes, her eyes wide as she watched the scene unfold. As we approached, she turned to face us, her face pale in the moonlight.

"Belinda," I began, my voice steady despite the turmoil inside me. "We need to talk."

She looked at us, her eyes darting between Thorn and me. "I didn't do anything," she said quickly. "I swear."

"We heard you were arguing with Isadora before the fireworks started," Thorn said, his voice stern but not unkind.

Belinda's face flushed. "Yes, we argued. But I didn't hurt her. I wouldn't..."

Her voice trailed off, and she looked away. There was bitterness in her eyes, but also fear and worry. It was clear that despite their argument, Belinda cared about Isadora.

"We're not accusing you," I said gently. "We just need to understand what happened."

Belinda nodded, her eyes still on the ground. "I understand," she said quietly. "I hope Isadora is okay."

Her sincerity was palpable, and I found myself believing her.

Belinda's voice was barely a whisper as she continued her story. "I... I had gone to the bathroom when it happened. I didn't see anything."

Her eyes were wide and fearful, her hands trembling slightly. It was clear that the events of the evening had shaken her.

"Did you notice anything unusual when you came back?" Thorn asked, his voice gentle. "Anyone acting suspiciously, or anything out of place?"

Belinda shook her head, her fiery hair swaying with the movement. "No, nothing. Everyone was just... panicking. I didn't know what had happened until I saw Isadora..."

Her voice broke, and she swallowed hard, her gaze dropping to her hands. I exchanged a glance with Thorn. Belinda's alibi seemed solid because she appeared to be being honest, but we still had more questions than answers.

"Thank you, Belinda," I said, my voice soft. "We appreciate your help."

As we left her there by the lake, I couldn't help but feel a pang of sympathy for the young witch. She was clearly upset, and I had no doubt that the night's events would haunt her for a long time to come.

Chapter Five

The hospital was a stark contrast to the vibrant festivities of the town square. The sterile smell of antiseptic hung heavy in the air, a constant reminder of the grim reality we were facing. Meri and I navigated the quiet corridors, our footsteps echoing off the linoleum floors as we made our way to Isadora's room.

Upon entering, we were met with a somber scene. Isadora's mother, a petite woman with a shock of white hair, sat by her daughter's bedside, her hands clasped tightly around Isadora's. Beside her, Isadora's cousin, a tall woman with the same fiery hair, stood with a look of quiet determination on her face.

As we stepped into the room, Isadora's mother looked up, her eyes red-rimmed from crying. Despite her evident distress, she managed a small, weary smile. "Kinsley," she greeted, her voice hoarse from what I assumed were hours of worry and tears. "Thank you for coming."

Her cousin echoed her sentiment, nodding in agreement. "It means a lot to us," she added, her voice steady.

Over the next hour, we found ourselves immersed in a quiet, intimate conversation with Isadora's family.

Her mother, a woman of gentle strength, began to share stories from Isadora's childhood. She spoke of a young girl with a boundless curiosity and a fascination for the magical world, a child who would spend hours poring over spell books and practicing incantations.

Her cousin, a woman who shared Isadora's fiery hair and fierce determination, chimed in with her own memories. She recounted tales of their shared adventures, of the countless hours they spent exploring the woods, searching for magical herbs and enchanted artifacts. She spoke of Isadora's unwavering dedication to her craft, of her tireless efforts to master her magical abilities.

As they spoke, I could see Isadora in their stories - the passionate, determined woman I knew. The conversation, though tinged with sadness, served as a welcome distraction from the grim reality of our situation. It was a testament to Isadora's spirit, a reminder of the vibrant, lively woman who lay fighting for her life in the hospital bed.

The stories flowed, each one painting a vivid picture of Isadora's life. They spoke of her love for the library, of the countless hours she spent among its shelves, lost in the world of books. They shared anecdotes of her unwavering dedication to her work, of the joy she found in sharing her love for magic with the town's residents.

Periodically, I would excuse myself from the conversation, rising from the hard plastic chair that had become my temporary perch. I would navigate the sterile hospital corridors, the hum of fluorescent lights overhead and the distant chatter of medical staff my only company as I made my way to the hospital cafeteria.

The cafeteria was a hub of activity, a stark contrast to the quiet solemnity of Isadora's room. Medical staff, visitors, and patients alike bustled about, their conversations a low murmur in the background. I joined the line, selecting a variety of snacks, sandwiches, and drinks before making my way to the counter to pay.

Returning to Isadora's room, I distributed the food and drinks, placing them on the small table by Isadora's bed. Isadora's mother offered a small, grateful smile, her hands wrapping around the warm coffee cup as if it were a lifeline. Her cousin thanked me, her gaze briefly leaving Isadora's still form to acknowledge the food.

It was a small gesture, a simple act of fetching food and drink. Yet, it seemed to provide a measure of comfort to Isadora's family. It was a tangible reminder that they were not alone in their vigil, that there were others who shared their concern, their fear, and their hope for Isadora's recovery. It was a small act of solidarity, a silent promise that we were there for them, and for Isadora, in any way we could be.

Just as I was gathering my thoughts to announce my departure, Isadora's cousin, Marianne, brought up a subject that piqued my interest.

"You know," she began, her gaze distant as she stared at the sterile white hospital walls, "Isadora is going to be devastated if this...incident sets back her plans for the library. She's been so excited about them lately."

I turned to her, curiosity piqued. "What plans?" I asked.

Marianne looked at me, her eyes reflecting a mixture of worry and determination. "She's been working on a project for the library. Something about expanding the magical section, making it more accessible to the younger witches and wizards in town. She's been trying to secure additional funding for it."

I felt a pang of surprise. "From Mayor Taylor?" I asked, remembering my earlier encounter with the man.

Marianne nodded. "Yes. But Miles...he's been less than enthusiastic about the idea. He doesn't see the value in it, I suppose. He and Isadora have been at odds over it for weeks now."

A knot formed in my stomach as I processed this new information. The tension between Isadora and the mayor, the strange magical residue on Isadora's clothes, and now this revelation about their disagreement over library funding. It was a lot to take in, and it added a new layer of complexity to the situation. I thanked Marianne for the information, promising to look into it, and left the hospital with my mind buzzing with questions.

The drive over to the sheriff's station was a quiet one, the radio on low was the only sound breaking the silence. Meri sat in the passenger seat, his golden eyes reflecting the glass as he gazed out the window. I could tell he was deep in thought, likely piecing together the same puzzle I was.

Upon arrival, I made my way to Thorn's office, Meri following behind me. Thorn was seated at his desk, his brow furrowed as he read through a stack of reports. He looked up as I entered, his expression softening as he took in my serious demeanor.

"Kinsley," he greeted, setting aside his paperwork. "What brings you here?"

I took a deep breath, gathering my thoughts before speaking. "I just came from the hospital. I spoke with Isadora's family."

Thorn's eyes narrowed slightly, his attention fully on me now. "And?"

I relayed the conversation I'd had with Marianne, detailing Isadora's plans for the library and her disagreements with Mayor Taylor. As I spoke, Thorn's expression grew more serious, his gaze never leaving mine.

"So, Isadora and the mayor were at odds over library funding," he mused, leaning back in his chair. "That's...interesting."

"It's more than interesting, Thorn," I replied, my tone firm. "It's a possible motive. We need to look into this."

"Okay, Kinsley, I'll head over to the mayor's office as soon as I wrap up what I was doing."

"Thorn," I began, my voice steady and resolute, "I want to accompany you when you question Mayor Taylor."

Thorn paused, his eyes meeting mine in a silent exchange. He seemed to be weighing the pros and cons of my request, his gaze thoughtful. After a moment, he gave a single nod of agreement. "All right, Kinsley," he conceded, "But remember, this is an official investigation. We need to tread carefully."

With our plan in place, we left the sheriff's station and embarked on the short drive to the town square. The familiar sights of Coventry passed by in a blur, the quaint buildings and bustling streets a stark contrast to the unease that hung in the air. As we parked and began our walk across the square towards the courthouse, I found myself instinctively looking up at the grand building.

My heart skipped a beat as I noticed a figure peering down at us from the top floor windows. The black-eyed ghost. I hadn't seen her in a while, and her sudden appearance sent a shiver down my spine. Was her presence a bad omen? The thought was unsettling, but I pushed it aside, focusing on the task at hand.

We entered the courthouse, the heavy doors closing behind us with a resounding thud. The mayor's secretary, a stern-looking woman with glasses perched precariously on the end of her nose, looked up as we approached. "The mayor is currently unavailable," she informed us, her tone leaving no room for argument.

Thorn, however, was not so easily deterred. "This is a matter of utmost importance," he insisted, his voice firm but respectful. "We need to speak with Mayor Taylor immediately."

The secretary hesitated, her gaze flicking between Thorn and me. The tension in the room was palpable as she deliberated, clearly torn between her loyalty to the mayor and the authority that Thorn carried as the town's sheriff. After what felt like an eternity, she finally relented, pressing a button on her desk that buzzed us through to the mayor's office.

As we made our way towards the office, I couldn't shake off the sense of apprehension that had settled over me.

The atmosphere in Mayor Taylor's office was thick with tension as Thorn and I took our seats across from him. The room was a testament to the mayor's taste, with its rich mahogany desk, plush leather chairs, and walls adorned with tasteful art. Meri, ever the silent observer, had taken up a position at my feet, his sharp eyes watching the mayor intently.

"Mayor Taylor," Thorn began, his tone professional yet firm. "We're here to discuss the incident involving Isadora at the fireworks display."

Mayor Taylor's eyebrows shot up in surprise. "Why would you be discussing that with me?" he asked, his voice laced with confusion.

"Because," I interjected, "Isadora was working on a project for the library that involved securing additional funding. We understand that you and she had been at odds over this."

The mayor's face remained impassive as he responded, "I heard about the unfortunate incident, but I assure you, I had no involvement in it."

His words rang hollow, especially when I took in his attire. He was dressed in a suit from Saville Rowe, its tailored fit and luxurious fabric a clear indicator of its high cost. A Rolex watch glinted on his wrist, its weighty presence a stark contrast to his claims of financial constraints.

"And yet," I said, my gaze fixed on the Rolex, "you're wearing a suit that costs more than some people's monthly salary and a watch that could fund a small library on its own."

The mayor shifted uncomfortably in his seat, his gaze flickering to his watch before meeting mine. "The town has financial constraints," he said, his voice firm. "It's not possible to expand the budget at this time."

The air in the mayor's office seemed to thicken, becoming almost palpable as Thorn leaned in slightly, his gaze steady on Mayor Taylor. "Mayor, could you tell us where you were during the time of Isadora's attack?" he asked, his tone professional and devoid of any accusation.

Mayor Taylor's reaction was immediate and intense. His face, previously a mask of polite indifference, flushed a deep, angry red. His eyes, a cold, icy blue, sparked with indignation and disbelief. He leaned back in his chair, his hands gripping the armrests tightly as if to anchor himself.

"Excuse me?" he sputtered, his voice echoing around the room. "Are you seriously asking me for an alibi, Sheriff? Is this what you consider police work?"

Thorn didn't flinch under the mayor's heated gaze. He simply nodded, his expression remaining calm and unyielding. "Yes, Mayor Taylor," he replied. "I'm asking for your alibi. It's standard procedure in an investigation."

The mayor's eyes flashed dangerously, his lips curling into a sneer. "Well, Sheriff," he spat, "I find it hard to believe that you don't have better things to do than harass me with these ridiculous questions."

Thorn remained unflappable, his calm demeanor a stark contrast to the mayor's growing agitation. "I'm doing my job, Mayor Taylor," he said evenly. "This isn't personal."

The mayor bristled at Thorn's words, his hands clenching into fists on the desk. "Perhaps I need to take a closer look at Coventry's budget," he retorted, his voice icy. "If our full-time sheriff has nothing better to do than... this." He waved a dismissive hand in our direction.

I felt a surge of anger at his words, and I leaned forward in my chair, my gaze locked with his. "Do I need to get my family involved, Mayor Taylor?" I asked, my voice low but firm.

The mayor's demeanor changed instantly. His anger seemed to deflate, replaced by a more subdued, almost chastised demeanor. He looked like a scolded dog, his tail between his legs.

"Fine," he grumbled, his voice barely above a whisper. "If you must know, I was hosting a party on the other side of the lake during the fireworks. There were many important, influential people there. They can vouch for me."

His words had a desperate edge to them, like a child seeking validation for a job well done. Thorn simply nodded, thanked him for his time, and extended his hand. The mayor shook it limply, his gaze avoiding ours as we left his office.

With our meeting with the mayor concluded, Thorn and I left the courthouse and made our way across the bustling town square. The library, a grand old building with a history as rich as the town itself, stood proudly at the far end. Its stone facade was weathered by time, but it still held an air of dignity and importance.

My family's connection to the library ran deep. Since its establishment, the head librarian had always been a member of our family. This gave us an unspoken authority and access that others didn't have. As we approached the entrance, I felt a sense of familiarity and comfort wash over me. The library was more than just a building; it was a part of our family's legacy.

We entered the library, the familiar scent of old books and polished wood filling my senses. The library was quiet, the usual hum of activity subdued in the wake of the day's events. We made our way to Isadora's office, tucked away in the back of the library. The door was slightly ajar, and we stepped inside, ready to delve into the mystery that had unfolded.

The office of Isadora was a testament to her character, a blend of meticulous organization and a touch of whimsy. Bookshelves lined the walls, a testament to her love of literature, both magical and mundane. Her desk was a controlled chaos of papers, books, and a half-drunk cup of tea, now cold.

Meri, ever the curious feline, hopped onto the desk, his gold eyes scanning the room with an air of nonchalance. "You know, if you're looking for dirt, I don't think you'll find it here," he quipped, his tail flicking lazily.

Ignoring his comment, I began to sift through the papers on Isadora's desk. Among the various documents, my eyes landed on a detailed proposal. It was a plan to create a new children's section in the library, a project that would undoubtedly require a significant amount of funding.

"Look at this," I said, holding up the proposal.

Meri glanced at it, his eyes narrowing slightly. "A new children's section? That's what all this fuss is about?"

"It's not just that, Meri," I replied, scanning the document. "This would require a lot of funding. The town treasury is listed as a potential source, but so are private donations."

Meri huffed, his whiskers twitching. "So, our dear mayor is more interested in his fancy suits than in the future of the town's children. Typical."

I couldn't help but agree. The mayor's refusal to expand the library's budget, his ostentatious lifestyle... it all seemed to fit together in a disturbing way. But we needed more evidence, more information.

As I leafed through the proposal, my eyes were drawn to the scrawled handwriting at the bottom of the last page. Isadora's notes, a stream of consciousness that flowed from her mind onto the paper. Her frustration with Mayor Taylor was evident in the sharpness of her words, the intensity of her script. But it was a particular name that caught my attention and caused me to pause.

"Meri," I called, my eyes still fixed on the paper. "Do you remember Richard Blackwell?"

Meri, who had been lounging on a nearby chair, perked up at the mention of the name. His gold eyes met mine, curiosity flickering within them. "Blackwell? Yeah, he's a businessman. Owns a bunch of properties around town. Why?"

I pointed to the name on the paper, my finger tracing the letters. "According to Isadora's notes, he had initially approached her about funding the new children's section. But it seems he's recently withdrawn his support."

Meri's tail twitched, a sure sign of his interest. He hopped off the chair and padded over to me, his eyes scanning the paper. "That's strange," he mused, his whiskers twitching. "Blackwell's always been a big supporter of community projects. It doesn't make sense for him to back out now."

"I agree," I replied, my mind whirling with questions. "It's definitely something we need to look into."

As I continued to read through Isadora's notes, I felt a sense of unease settle over me. There was more to this situation than met the eye, and I had a feeling we were only scratching the surface. But what lay beneath? That was the question we needed to answer.

Thorn's return to Isadora's office was marked by a quiet sigh, his expression one of mild frustration. "No luck," he admitted, running a hand through his hair. "Everyone I spoke to adores Isadora. Only half of them even knew she was a witch. The others... well, they work on the mundane side of the library. They're oblivious to the world of magic."

I nodded, not surprised. The library had always been a place where the magical and mundane coexisted, albeit with a thin veil of secrecy separating the two. "Take a look at this," I said, handing him the proposal I had found. "It's Isadora's plan for a new children's section in the magical wing of the library."

Thorn accepted the document, his brows furrowing as he began to read. I watched him, noting the way his eyes moved across the page, the slight furrow of his brow deepening as he absorbed the information. The room was silent save for the distant hum of the library beyond the office door, the quiet punctuated only by the occasional rustle of paper as Thorn turned the pages.

After a few minutes, he looked up, his gaze meeting mine. "This is ambitious," he said, a note of admiration in his voice. "A whole new section dedicated to children's magic literature. It's a great idea. But it would require a lot of funding."

I nodded, pointing to Isadora's notes at the end of the proposal. "She had a potential donor. Richard Blackwell. But according to these notes, he recently pulled his support."

Thorn's expression shifted, a thoughtful frown tugging at his lips. "Blackwell, huh? That's interesting. We should definitely look into that. Blackwell might have been coerced into withdrawing his support," he finally said, his voice thoughtful. He looked up from the proposal, meeting my gaze with a serious expression. "There could be someone who stands to gain from keeping the library's funding low."

I felt a chill run down my spine at his words. "But who would benefit from that?" I asked, my mind racing to make sense of the puzzle pieces we had. "And why would they go to such lengths?"

Thorn shrugged, his expression tightening. "There could be a multitude of reasons. Perhaps they're against the library expanding its influence, or they're concerned about the spread of magic in the community. It could even be something more personal."

My thoughts immediately went to Isadora, to the vision of her engulfed in flames. "You mean, like a vendetta against Isadora?" I suggested, my voice barely above a whisper.

"Possibly," Thorn conceded, his gaze never leaving mine. "We need to dig deeper into Blackwell's decision to pull his support. We also need to find out if there's anyone else who might have had a motive to harm Isadora."

"Richard Blackwell," Thorn mused, rolling the name around in his mouth as if tasting it. "He's our next stop."

I nodded in agreement, my mind already racing ahead to the upcoming interview. Richard was a prominent figure in Coventry, his name synonymous with a myriad of business ventures that reached far beyond the town's borders. Yet, despite his widespread interests, he had always maintained a strong presence in Coventry, including an office space right in the heart of town.

"He's got his fingers in a lot of pies," I remarked, "but he's always had a soft spot for Coventry. It's where he started, after all."

Thorn nodded, his gaze thoughtful. "True. And that's why his sudden withdrawal from the library project is so... odd. It doesn't fit."

A silence fell between us, both lost in our thoughts. The library project was something that would benefit the community, something that Richard had initially been eager to support. His sudden change of heart was puzzling, to say the least.

"Let's pay him a visit," Thorn finally suggested, breaking the silence. "See if we can get some answers."

As we exited the library, Thorn pulled out his phone. He dialed a number, his expression focused as he waited for the call to connect. I could only catch snippets of the conversation, but it was enough to confirm that Richard was indeed in his office today.

"Thank you, we'll be there shortly," Thorn concluded, ending the call and slipping his phone back into his pocket. He glanced at me,. "Richard's in. Let's go."

We made our way to Thorn's cruiser, parked a short distance away. He held the door for me as if we were on a date. Meri jumped in too and settled in on the seat beside me.

As Thorn and I stepped into the polished interior of Richard Blackwell's office, it was immediately apparent that his secretary hadn't been expecting us to actually show up. Her eyes widened in surprise, and she quickly stood from her desk, her usual professional demeanor momentarily slipping in the face of our unexpected arrival.

"Sheriff Wilson, Mrs. Wilson," she stammered, her gaze darting between us. "I wasn't aware you were planning to visit. Please, let me inform Mr. Blackwell of your arrival."

With that, she swiftly retreated into the inner sanctum of Richard's office, leaving Thorn and me in the sleek, modern reception area. The space was a testament to Richard's success, filled with expensive furniture, tasteful artwork, and an air of quiet confidence.

We waited in silence, the only sound the soft whoosh of the air conditioning and the muffled murmur of a couple having a conversation outside the office windows. After a few tense minutes, the secretary reappeared, her face slightly flushed from her hurried conversation with Richard.

"Mr. Blackwell will see you now," she announced, gesturing towards the imposing office door. "But please be aware, he only has a few minutes."

We thanked her for her assistance and made our way into Richard's office.

As we entered Richard's office, the man himself rose from behind a large mahogany desk, his face breaking into a polite smile. He extended a hand to Thorn first, then to me, his grip firm and confident. Meri, ever the silent observer, padded in after us, settling at my feet without drawing any attention from Richard. I found myself wondering just how much Richard knew about the magical side of Coventry. After all, he had been willing to fund a magical children's section in the library. But then again, he might just be an unsuspecting benefactor.

"Good to see you, Sheriff Wilson, Mrs. Wilson," Richard greeted, his voice smooth and controlled. "I've heard a lot about you and your family," he said to me. "Your names carry quite a reputation in Coventry."

His words were a reminder of the influence my family held in the town, a fact that was both a blessing and a curse at times. He gestured towards the luxurious chairs in front of his desk, inviting us to sit. We took our seats, the soft leather creaking slightly under our weight.

"Now, how can I assist you today?" Richard asked, leaning back in his chair, his gaze shifting between Thorn and me. His demeanor was calm, but there was a hint of curiosity in his eyes. He was clearly wondering why the town's sheriff had decided to pay him a visit.

"Mr. Blackwell," Thorn began, leaning back in his chair, his gaze steady on the businessman. "We're here to discuss the library project. We understand you were a significant contributor, but you've recently withdrawn your support. Can you tell us why?"

Richard shifted in his seat, his fingers drumming a rhythm on the polished surface of his desk. "Yes, that's correct," he admitted, his voice steady. "I did pull out of the project."

"Any particular reason?" I asked, trying to keep my tone casual.

Richard sighed, his gaze drifting to the window for a moment before returning to us. "I've been dealing with some personal issues lately," he confessed. "It's made me reconsider some of my financial commitments."

Thorn and I exchanged a glance. "Personal issues?" Thorn echoed, his tone neutral. "Anything that might be related to the library or Isadora?"

Richard shook his head, a hint of irritation flashing in his eyes. "No, nothing like that. It's... well, it's personal. I'd rather not discuss it."

"Understandable," Thorn replied, his tone still calm. "But we have to ask, Mr. Blackwell. Were you pressured or threatened in any way to withdraw your support?"

Richard's eyes widened slightly, and he seemed taken aback by the question. "Threatened? No, not at all," he said, shaking his head emphatically. "This decision was entirely my own."

"Mr. Blackwell," I began, my tone gentle but firm. "I understand that you're dealing with personal matters. But Isadora is in the hospital right now, gravely injured. We need to understand what happened to her."

Richard's face paled slightly, and he looked down at his hands. "I... I understand," he said, his voice barely above a whisper. "It's just... it's been a difficult time."

"I can see that," I said, my voice softening. "But it's curious to me that you withdrew your financial support of her library project right before she was hurt."

Richard's eyes flicked up to meet mine, and I could see the surprise in them. He opened his mouth to respond, then closed it again, seeming to struggle with his words. Finally, he sighed and ran a hand through his hair. "All right," he said, his voice heavy. "You're right. I owe you an explanation."

He took a deep breath, then began to speak. "A member of my family has been... gambling. A lot. And my wife, she took out a bunch of credit cards to remodel our house instead of getting a low-interest loan. And my father... he's been sick. I've been carrying a lot of his debt too."

He paused, his gaze dropping to his hands again. "Is that a good enough reason?" he asked, his voice barely audible.

I felt a pang of sympathy for the man. It was clear he was dealing with a lot. "I'm sorry to hear that, Richard," I said sincerely. "And I apologize for prying. But I hope you understand why we had to ask."

Richard sighed and nodded. "I do," he said, his voice heavy. "I've been beside myself about Isadora. She's such a good woman. I'm glad to do anything I can to help figure out what happened to her."

"Thank you for your candor, Richard," Thorn said, rising from his chair. "If you think of anything else that might help, please don't hesitate to give me a call."

Richard nodded, standing as well. We shook hands again, the atmosphere in the room significantly lighter than it had been when we arrived.

"I think I'll go visit Isadora at the hospital," Richard said, his voice thoughtful. "See if her family needs anything. I might not be able to fund her library project right now, but I can at least extend my help to them."

I smiled at him, touched by his offer. "I think they'll appreciate that more than you know, Richard."

With that, Thorn, Meri, and I left Richard's office, leaving him to his thoughts. As we walked away, I felt a little better. We hadn't found the answers we were looking for, but we had at least ruled out one potential suspect. And in the process, we had perhaps helped a family in need.

Chapter Six

The hospital was unusually quiet when I arrived early the next morning. The typical hustle and bustle of the place was muted, replaced by a hushed stillness that seemed to echo the gravity of Isadora's condition. As I walked through the sterile corridors, my footsteps echoed ominously, the sound bouncing off the cold, hard tiles.

I was met by a nurse who I recognized as Agate Skeenbauer. She was a member of one of the oldest witch families in Coventry, and her face was etched with concern as she greeted me.

"Isadora's in surgery," she informed me, her voice barely above a whisper. The news hit me like a punch in the gut, and I could only nod in response. Agate continued, "Her cousin is at her house, looking after her daughter."

I thanked her for the information, my mind racing with worry for Isadora and her family. But then Agate said something that caught me off guard.

"It's a shame about our magic being weaker," she said, her gaze dropping to the floor. "If it weren't for... well, you know... we could have healed Isadora's injuries."

Her words hung in the air between us, a stark reminder of the sacrifice I'd made to bring Meri back from the dead. A sacrifice that had weakened our magic. A pang of guilt washed over me, but I quickly pushed it aside. I knew I'd made the right choice, even if it had unforeseen consequences.

"I... I'm sorry," Agate stammered, her cheeks flushing with embarrassment. "I shouldn't have said that."

I forced a smile, trying to reassure her. "It's okay," I said, my voice steady. "I understand."

With that, Meri and I made our way to Isadora's room. Her mother was there, slumped in a chair by her bed, fast asleep. The sight of her, so worn and weary, tugged at my heartstrings. Not wanting to disturb her, we quietly retreated from the room, leaving the hospital and returning to my car.

In the car, Meri and I sat quietly, the hum of the radio turned down to low the only sound breaking the silence. The hospital loomed in the rearview mirror as I mulled over our next steps.

"Perhaps we should revisit the lake," Meri suggested, breaking the silence. His tone was casual, but his eyes were serious. "The mundane law enforcement might have missed something."

I glanced at him, considering his words. "You think we should use a bit of magic to aid our investigation?" I asked, a hint of a smile playing on my lips.

Meri snorted, his tail flicking in amusement. "Well, it's not like we can rely on your baking skills to solve this mystery," he retorted, his whiskers twitching in a feline grin.

I laughed, the tension in the car easing a bit. "All right, Detective Meri," I said, turning the car in the direction of the lake. "Let's see what we can find."

As I navigated the car towards the lake, Meri's tail flicked to the rhythm of a catchy tune playing on the radio. The tension from the hospital visit was still palpable, but our playful banter was a welcome diversion.

"So, are we turning the lake into a giant espresso?" Meri quipped, his eyes sparkling with mischief. "That should perk up any dormant clues."

I laughed, shaking my head. "Meri."

"Hey, it's worth a shot," he shot back, a smirk playing on his feline lips. "Your magic has pulled off stranger stunts."

"Touché," I conceded, grinning at his audacity. "But let's stick to the less caffeinated methods for now."

As we neared the lake, Meri's tail twitched in thought. "You know, we could always summon a ghost to tell us what happened," he suggested, his tone casual.

I shot him a disapproving look. "Meri, Isadora is still alive. That's not a nice thing to say."

He rolled his eyes, a distinctly human gesture that always seemed out of place on his feline face. "I wasn't talking about Isadora. This town is crawling with ghosts, watching everyone's every move. They're like the supernatural neighborhood watch."

I raised an eyebrow at him. "Are you seriously suggesting I summon a ghost?"

He let out a snort of laughter. "Oh, no. I was just joking. I know you mess it up every time you try to summon a ghost. Remember the time you accidentally summoned that banshee instead of Great-Aunt Ethel?"

"I was a kid when that happened, and you swore secrecy." I couldn't help but laugh at the memory. "All right, all right. Keep it up, and I might just forget how to summon your lunch when we're done here."

Meri's eyes widened in mock horror. "You wouldn't dare."

The small parking lot adjacent to the park was unusually quiet when we arrived. The usual hum of

76

activity was absent, the park's typical visitors likely deterred by the unsettling events of the previous night. Meri and I stepped out of the car, the crisp morning air carrying the scent of dew-kissed grass and the faint, earthy aroma of the lake. The tranquility of the scene was a stark contrast to the chaos that had unfolded here just hours ago.

We began our investigation, our magic extending outwards like invisible tendrils, probing the area for any signs of disturbance. Meri, with his keen feline senses and innate magical intuition, prowled the perimeter of the park. His eyes were sharp, his movements precise as he navigated the landscape. Meanwhile, I focused my attention on the edge of the lake, the epicenter of the incident. My magic swept over the area, a silent sentinel seeking any traces of magical residue or anomalies.

Time seemed to stretch on as we methodically combed through the park. The silence was punctuated only by the occasional rustle of leaves or the distant call of a bird. Then, without warning, Meri's ears perked up. His body tensed, his gaze locked onto a patch of brush near the water's edge. I followed his line of sight...

Hidden under the brush, half-submerged in the water, was a small potion bottle. It was empty, but faint traces of magic still clung to it. The residue was a sickly yellow color, eerily similar to the residue I had found on Isadora's clothes. It was a chilling discovery, suggesting that the attacker might have used a potion to enhance their spellcasting abilities.

I carefully picked up the bottle using a conjured cloth, mindful not to contaminate any potential magical fingerprints. Meri looked up at me, his eyes reflecting the seriousness of our discovery. "This could be a significant lead, Meri," I murmured, tucking the potion bottle safely into my bag. "This suggests that our attacker didn't just rely on their innate magic. They used a potion to boost their abilities."

Meri's tail flicked in agreement. "This investigation just got a lot more complicated, didn't it?"

"Not as complicated as if I'd blown something up, right?"

"Whatever."

"Whatever, cat. Let's get some food and then find out what was in this potion."

"All you had to say was food..."

***

"How about Popeye's?" I suggested, already picturing the crispy chicken sandwich that had become a fast favorite of mine. "They've got that new sandwich with cheese and bacon."

78

Meri's ears perked up at the mention of bacon. "Fine," he replied. "Just hold the bun on mine. I don't eat bread like a savage."

"First of all, you do eat bread. Second of all, Bonkers isn't a savage. He's your friend."

"I do not consent."

"Let's just get something to eat," I said and scratched behind his ear.

With our lunch destination decided, I steered the car towards the new section of Coventry where the recently opened Popeye's was located. The smell of fried chicken filled the air as we pulled into the drive-through lane, making my stomach growl in anticipation.

After placing our order at the speaker, we pulled forward to the window to pay. As the window slid open, I was met with a sight that made my breath hitch in my throat. The young woman working the window had hair so sapphire blue it was almost black. It was the same shade I'd seen in my shop's security footage, the same shade that had been on the woman who'd left the shapeshifting spell.

Caught off guard, I must have been staring because the woman asked, "Are you okay?" Her voice was filled with genuine concern, but I could only stammer out a quick affirmation.

As she closed the window, Meri chided me, "Keep it cool, will you? That hair color is all the rage these days. Remember when you hair, and Brighton's, used to turn all sorts of weird colors? It's a thing. Doesn't mean she's…"

"It doesn't means she's Agent Smith," I nodded, trying to regain my composure. Meri was right, of course. "Besides, why would he get a job at Popeye's? And how would he know I'd come here? I'm just being paranoid." But when the window slid open again and the woman handed me our food, she winked at me. It was a small gesture, but it sent a chill down my spine. Was I really being paranoid?

I pulled into a parking spot, my mind racing. "I'm going inside," I announced, already unbuckling my seatbelt. Meri let out a low growl of protest.

"Chill out," he advised. "You'll sound like a lunatic if you confront her about a video where her face keeps shifting. Plus, it's not concrete proof it's her, because of the whole face-shifting thing."

I sighed, sinking back into my seat. Meri was right, again.

The Popeye's chicken sandwiches were as delicious as I remembered, but I couldn't fully enjoy mine. My gaze kept drifting back to the drive-through window, half-expecting to see the sapphire-haired woman again. But she never reappeared, and if it weren't for Meri's confirmation, I might have convinced myself that I'd imagined her.

Once we finished our meal, I decided it was time to pay a visit to Lilith. If there was anyone in Coventry who could identify the potion we'd found, it was her. She was the foremost expert on illicit potions... and well any kind of "questionable" magic.

As we pulled into the driveway, I could hear strange noises coming from inside the house. There was a peculiar smell in the air, too, something I couldn't quite place. I rang the doorbell, and after a moment, the door creaked open to reveal Lilith.

She was dressed entirely in black, her gray hair piled into a loose bun atop her head. The strange smell was stronger now, and the odd noises continued in the background.

"Lilith, I need your help with something," I said, holding up the potion bottle. "Is this a bad time?"

She looked at me, then back into her house, and shouted, "You better shut up or I'll send you back to the bad place!" The noises immediately ceased, replaced by a faint whimper.

With a satisfied nod, Lilith turned back to me. "Of course it's not a bad time," she said, stepping aside to let us in. The smell had dissipated, and the house was now eerily quiet.

As we stepped inside, I couldn't help but ask about the strange occurrence. "What was that all about?"

Lilith simply shrugged, a mischievous glint in her eye. "It's better not to know," she said, leading us further into her home.

"Have you heard about what happened to Isadora?" I asked, taking a seat on one of the chairs.

Lilith nodded, her face serious. "Yes, I heard. I would have been at the festival, but I had... business... to attend to." She left the room, returning a moment later with two bottles of soda - a regular Coke for me and a Diet Coke for herself.

I always found it odd that Lilith drank diet soda. As witches, we didn't have to worry about things like calories. But Lilith once told me she liked the idea of something so sweet it was bitter.

Turning my attention back to the matter at hand, I reached into my bag and pulled out the potion bottle Meri and I had discovered at the lake. I handed it to Lilith, watching as her eyes narrowed in concentration. She held the bottle up to the light, her gaze intense as she examined the contents.

Lilith's eyes flickered to mine, her gaze serious. "Are you certain you want to know what's in this?" she asked, gesturing to the bottle in her hand.

I nodded, my curiosity piqued. "Yes, but why do you ask?"

She sighed, setting the bottle down on a nearby table. "I have a suspicion about what this might be, and if I'm right, it's not good news."

I raised an eyebrow at her. "Worse than the stuff you dabble in?" I asked, trying to lighten the mood with a bit of humor.

Lilith shot me a look that was half-amused, half-annoyed. "I don't dabble," she retorted, her tone dry. Then, her expression turned serious again. "Wait here," she instructed, standing up from her chair. "Meri, come with me."

I started to rise, intending to follow them. "I want to come too," I protested, but Lilith held up a hand to stop me.

"No, stay put," she insisted, her voice firm. There was an edge to her tone that I hadn't heard before, a warning that whatever she was about to do might be dangerous. I hesitated, then nodded, settling back into my chair.

As Lilith and Meri disappeared into another room, I was left alone in the parlor. I could only guess that they were headed to the dining room. Lilith often used the large table there to spread out her tools when she was working on something particularly complex. I took a deep breath, trying to quell the anxiety that had settled in my stomach.

The noises emanating from the other room were a symphony of the unexpected. It started with a soft fizzing, akin to the sound of a carbonated drink being uncapped. This was followed by a series of pops, like a string of tiny firecrackers being set off. The crescendo was a loud bang that made me jump in my seat, my heart pounding in response to the sudden noise. The finale was a chorus of colorful language from both Lilith and Meri, their voices echoing through the old Victorian house.

The urge to rise from my seat and investigate was strong, but I remembered Lilith's stern instruction to stay put. So, I remained in the parlor, my fingers nervously drumming on my phone as I sought distraction in a game of *Candy Crush*. The minutes felt like they stretched into hours.

Finally, after what felt like an eternity, the door to the other room creaked open and Lilith and Meri emerged. Lilith's face was set in a serious expression, her brows furrowed in deep thought. "The potion," she began, her voice heavy with gravity, "contains a rare herb. One that the coven outlawed many years ago due to its unpredictable and dangerous effects."

I blinked in surprise at her revelation. "But we allow all kinds of poisonous plants to be used in our potions," I protested, my mind struggling to make sense of her words.

Lilith nodded in agreement. "Yes, we do. But this herb is different. It's so dangerous and unpredictable that the coven decided it was best to keep it away from Coventry's witches. That's why you've never heard of it." She paused for a moment, then added, "Even I don't use it."

Lilith's confession struck a nerve, sending an icy shiver skittering down my spine. She was a witch of considerable prowess, known far and wide for her audacious and unorthodox practices in magic. The fact that she, of all people, avoided this herb was a testament to its perilous nature.

I thanked Lilith for her help. She nodded, her eyes serious, and wished me luck. As I left her house, the grand Victorian looming ominously behind me, I couldn't help but feel a chill despite the warm summer air. Meri, ever the silent companion, padded alongside me. I opened the driver's side door, and he hopped in ahead of me.

The drive to the sheriff's station was quiet, the usual banter between Meri and me replaced by a tense silence. The streets of Coventry passed by in a blur.

As I parked the car outside the station, I took a moment to gather my thoughts. The information we had unearthed was significant, and I needed to present it to Thorn in a way that would make sense within the context of our investigation. Thorn was aware of the existence of magic, but the intricacies and nuances of our world were still largely outside of his wheelhouse. Taking a deep breath, I stepped out of the car, Meri at my heels, and headed towards the station.

Stepping into Thorn's office, I was greeted by the sight of him hunched over his desk, his brow furrowed in deep thought as he pored over case files. He looked up as I entered, his eyes curious. Meri immediately jumped onto the spare chair, curling up and watching us with keen interest.

"Thorn," I began, taking a seat across from him. "Meri and I found something at the lake. A potion bottle, hidden under some brush and half-submerged in the water."

Thorn looked up, his eyes narrowing slightly. "A potion bottle? You think it's connected to Isadora's attack?"

"I'm not sure," I admitted, "but it's a lead. We took it to Lilith for analysis."

Thorn's eyebrows shot up at that. "Lilith? How's the old demon queen doing?"

I couldn't help but chuckle at his choice of words. "She seems good. She was up to shenanigans when we got there, but she stopped whatever weird spell work she was doing to help me. Anyway, she found that the potion contains a rare herb, one that's been outlawed by the coven for years due to its unpredictable effects."

"Outlawed?" Thorn echoed, his expression serious. "Even by the coven's standards?"

I nodded, "Yes, it's that dangerous. Even Lilith, who isn't exactly known for her caution, doesn't use it."

Thorn leaned back in his chair, processing the information. After a moment, he looked at me, his gaze serious. "We need to talk to Isabella."

"Isadora's daughter?"

"Yes," Thorn confirmed. "I've been putting it off, considering the trauma she must be going through with her mother's injuries. But, I need to talk to her. And she might know something about this potion, or at least have some insight into her mother's work that we're not aware of."

I sighed, running a hand through my hair. "You're right," I admitted. "It's not ideal, but we need every piece of information we can get. Let's go talk to her."

Chapter Seven

The house of Isadora and Isabella was a testament to their lineage of fire witches. Nestled in a quiet corner of Coventry, the house was a beautiful Victorian structure, with a warm, red brick exterior that seemed to glow in the afternoon sun. The windows were adorned with stained glass, depicting intricate flame patterns that danced with the light. A large, ornate chimney towered over the house, a nod to their fire-wielding heritage. The front yard was a riot of colors, with a garden full of vibrant, heat-loving plants that thrived under Isadora's care.

As we approached the house, I could feel a gentle warmth radiating from it, a testament to the magic that resided within its walls. Thorn knocked on the door, and after a moment, it was opened by Isabella. The young witch looked tired and worried, but she managed a small smile as she invited us in.

Once inside, we were led to a cozy living room, where a fire crackled in the hearth despite the warm weather outside. Thorn and I took a seat, while Isabella perched on the edge of an armchair, wringing her hands nervously.

Thorn cleared his throat, breaking the silence that had settled in the room. "Isabella," he began, his voice gentle, "we're here because we're trying to piece together what happened to your mother. We found a potion bottle near the scene of the incident, and we were wondering if you might have seen anyone drop it. Or maybe you saw someone doing magic you didn't recognize?"

Isabella's brows furrowed as she considered Thorn's words. She shook her head slowly, her dark eyes filled with confusion and concern. "No," she said. "I didn't see anything like that. I was at the fireworks show, but I was with my friends, not near Mom."

She paused, biting her lower lip as if contemplating whether to continue. "But," she added, her voice gaining a bit of strength, "there is something else that's been bothering me."

Thorn and I exchanged a glance, our interest piqued. "Go on," I encouraged her, leaning forward in my seat.

Isabella took a deep breath before continuing, "A family heirloom has gone missing recently. It's... well, it's a bit macabre, but it's the skull of a witch who died during the Salem witch trials. It's been in our family for generations."

I raised an eyebrow at this but didn't interrupt. Isabella continued, "I know it sounds strange, but it's a powerful magical artifact. Mom was really upset when she couldn't find it. She was determined to find it."

I nodded, taking in this new information. "I understand," I said, "but you should know that warlocks have been known to use skulls as familiars. It's a bit suspicious, don't you think?"

Isabella shook her head quickly, her eyes wide. "No, it's nothing like that," she insisted. "The skull isn't a familiar. It's not sentient or anything like that. It's just... it's a part of our family history, and it's important to us."

Isabella's gaze dropped to her hands, her fingers twisting together in her lap. "There's more," she said, her voice barely above a whisper. "Mom... she's been acting strange lately. Nervous, like she's constantly looking over her shoulder."

Thorn and I exchanged a glance. "Can you elaborate?" he asked, his tone gentle.

Isabella nodded, her brow furrowed in thought. "She seemed like she wanted to tell me something. There were several times when she'd start to say something, then stop herself. It was like she was wrestling with whether or not to confide in me."

I leaned back in my chair, my mind racing. This was a new piece of the puzzle, and it could potentially be a significant one. "Did she give any indication of what she might have been wanting to discuss?" I asked.

Isabella shook her head, her expression filled with regret. "No, she never did. I wish... I wish I'd pushed her to tell me. Maybe I could have helped her."

As we left Isabella's house, the atmosphere in the car was thick with the weight of the information we had just received. The house, with its warm hues and flickering fireplaces, had been a stark contrast to the chilling news we had uncovered. The missing family heirloom, the skull of a Salem witch, was a piece of the puzzle we hadn't expected.

Thorn's cruiser hummed to life, the low rumble of the engine echoing the tension that hung between us. We sat in silence, each lost in our thoughts, the only sound the soft ticking of the car's indicator as Thorn navigated the familiar streets of Coventry.

The sudden buzz of Thorn's phone shattered the silence. He glanced at the screen, his brows furrowing as he answered the call. "Sheriff Wilson speaking," he said, his tone professional yet warm. I watched him, my curiosity piqued as his expression shifted from confusion to interest.

"We'll be right there," he said, ending the call abruptly. He turned to me, his eyes serious. "We've got a lead," he said, his voice steady. "A witness claims to have seen a suspicious person near the fireworks area before the incident. We need to head back to the station."

The drive back to the station was a blur, my mind racing with possibilities. Who could this suspicious person be? Could they be connected to the potion bottle we'd found? The questions swirled in my mind, each one leading to another, creating a web of uncertainty.

As we pulled into the parking lot at the station, I noticed a woman standing near the entrance, her posture rigid with anxiety. She was of medium build, her hair a soft shade of brown streaked with gray, and her eyes, a warm hazel, darted around nervously.

We exited the cruiser, and Thorn led the way towards the woman. As we approached, she straightened up, her eyes meeting ours with a mixture of apprehension and determination. Thorn extended his hand in greeting, introducing himself and then me.

"Mrs. Hopper, I'm Sheriff Wilson, and this is Mrs. Wilson," he said, his voice steady and reassuring.

"Please, call me Charlie," she replied, shaking our hands with a firm, albeit shaky grip. Her voice was soft, yet there was a hardness to it that hinted at something unreadable beneath her nervous exterior. "Charlie Hopper."

Charlie Hopper. The name didn't ring any bells for either of us. She was a stranger in a town where everyone knew everyone, which made her presence at the station all the more intriguing.

We led her to an interview room, a small, nondescript space with a single table and a few chairs. Charlie took a seat across from us, her hands clasped tightly in her lap.

As Thorn began the interview, I couldn't help but study her. Her face was kind, lined with the gentle signs of age, and her eyes held a certain sadness that made me wonder about her story. What had brought her here, to this room, with information that could potentially help us solve the mystery surrounding Isadora's attack?

Charlie took a deep breath, her fingers nervously twisting the hem of her blouse as she began to speak. Her voice was soft, but steady, as she recounted the events of that day.

"I was there early, you see," she started, her gaze focused on a spot on the table. "I like to get a good spot for the fireworks, away from the crowds. I was setting up my blanket when I noticed someone... odd."

She paused, her brow furrowing as she tried to recall the details. "They were standing near the area where the fireworks were being set up. They didn't seem to be part of the crew, and they weren't setting up for the show like the rest of us. They were just... lurking."

Her hands moved as she spoke, sketching out the scene in the air between us. "They were dressed in dark clothes, a hoodie, I think, even though it was warm out. And they kept looking around, like they were nervous or... or guilty."

Charlie's words hung in the air, her description painting a picture of a figure that seemed out of place amidst the festive preparations. It was vague, yes, but it was a lead - a person of interest who might have been involved in the incident.

"Did you see this person with anything like this?" Thorn asked, showing her a picture of the potion bottle.

Charlie shook her head. "No, I didn't see them with anything like that."

We thanked Charlie for her help, promising to follow up on her lead. As we stood to leave, Thorn asked Charlie to stay put for a few minutes. I was about to ask why when Thorn turned to me.

"Kinsley, could you run over to the Brew Station and grab us some coffee and pastries?" he asked.

I nodded, leaving the room and heading out to the Brew Station, my mind still buzzing with the new information we'd gathered.

With a bag of warm croissants in one hand and a tray of lattes in the other, I made my way back to the station. The aroma of the freshly brewed coffee and the buttery pastries filled the air.

Before heading back to the interview room, I stopped in the lobby to give Meri his bacon. He took it with a grateful chirp, settling down to enjoy his treat. He didn't mind not being in the interview room, as he would have found the whole thing boring. I was actually surprised he hadn't take off somewhere, but I suspected that the station receptionist had been feeding him some of her snack.

As I walked into Thorn's office, I found him hunched over his computer, his brow furrowed in concentration. I set his latte down on his desk, the steam curling up from the tiny opening in the lid.

"Thanks," he said, not taking his eyes off the screen. I leaned over to see what he was looking at. It was a file on Charlie Hopper.

"I did some digging while you were gone," he began, scrolling through the document. "Charlie's new in town, moved here a couple of months ago. And she has a record."

He clicked on a link, bringing up a list of charges. Theft, assault, a few other minor offenses. My heart sank a little. It was disappointing to think that our witness might not be as innocent as she seemed.

"But," Thorn continued, "that doesn't necessarily mean she's involved in this. She could just be a witness who happened to be in the wrong place at the wrong time. We'll need to dig deeper to find out for sure."

As Thorn and I re-entered the interview room, I balanced a tray of lattes and a bag of warm, flaky croissants from the Brew Station in my hands. Charlie Hopper, the woman we were about to question again, sat nervously at the table, her eyes darting between us. I could only guess that it never occurred to her that Thorn might be looking into her background, and that perhaps she should have just gotten up and left...

But then again, if she was that smart, maybe she wouldn't have come to the sheriff's station to give a tip in the first place. "Charlie," I began, setting the tray down on the table and sliding a latte and a croissant towards her. "We thought you might need a little pick-me-up."

She looked surprised but managed a small smile, murmuring a thank you as she wrapped her hands around the warm cup.

Thorn took a seat across from her, his expression serious. "We've been looking into your background, Charlie," he said, his voice steady but not unkind. "We know about your past."

Her eyes widened slightly, but she didn't seem shocked. Instead, she nodded, her fingers tightening around the cup. "I figured you might," she admitted. "But I swear, I didn't have anything to do with what happened to Isadora."

"We're not accusing you," I quickly added, hoping to ease her obvious anxiety. "We're just trying to understand everything that happened."

Charlie nodded, her gaze flicking between Thorn and me. "I understand," she said, her voice barely more than a whisper. "But I really didn't see anything else. I just saw that person lurking around."

Thorn sighed, running a hand over his face. "All right, Charlie. We believe you. But we may need to talk to you again if we have more questions."

She nodded, relief washing over her features. "Of course. Anything to help."

"You can't leave town yet, either."

"I couldn't if I wanted to," she admitted. "I'm afraid Coventry is the end of the line for me… at least until I can find a way… a legal way, to make some more money. What I'm saying is, don't worry about me flying the coop, because I'm stuck."

With that, we ended the interview. Despite her past, Thorn couldn't hold Charlie without more evidence, so we let her go.

Chapter Eight

Meri and I found ourselves heading back towards Isadora's house. Our day had been filled with interviews, investigations, and a constant search for answers. Yet, amidst all the chaos, I felt a pull to check in on Isabella. The poor girl was dealing with so much, and I wanted to offer her some comfort, away from the prying eyes of law enforcement.

Isadora's house was a warm beacon in the encroaching twilight, its windows glowing with soft light. As we approached, I could see Isabella through the front window, sitting alone in the living room. She looked up as we knocked, and a small smile of relief crossed her face as she opened the door to let us in.

"Mrs. Wilson, Meri," she greeted, stepping aside to let us in. "I wasn't expecting you. Is everything okay?"

"We're not here on official business," I reassured her, stepping inside. "I just wanted to check in on you, see if you needed anything."

Isabella's smile widened a fraction, and she led us into the living room. We sat down, and I asked her about her day, about how she was coping. She shared her worries, her fears, and I listened, offering words of comfort where I could.

As our conversation meandered, Isabella mentioned something that caught my attention. "Mom kept a journal," she said, her voice barely above a whisper. "She wrote in it every day. Maybe it could help you figure out what happened."

Meri's ears perked up at this, his eyes gleaming with interest. "A journal? That could be very useful. Do you know where it is?"

Isabella nodded, rising from her seat. "I think it's in her room. I can get it for you."

We waited in silence as Isabella disappeared down the hallway. A few minutes later, she returned, a worn leather-bound book in her hands. She handed it to me, her expression solemn.

"Please be careful with it," she said. "It is very important to her."

I nodded, cradling the journal in my hands. "We will, Isabella. Thank you." As we prepared to leave, I turned back to Isabella. "Isabella, is there anything else you need right now?" I asked, my voice soft. "Anything at all?"

She hesitated, her gaze dropping to the floor. "I... I want to see my mom," she admitted, her voice barely above a whisper. "But my grandmother... she says it's not a good idea. That I shouldn't see her like this."

I nodded, understanding the protective instinct that was likely driving her grandmother's decision. But Isabella was not a child, and she had a right to see her mother. "I'll have the Aunties talk to your grandmother," I promised. "They might be able to help."

Isabella's eyes brightened a fraction, a glimmer of hope sparking within them. "Thank you, Mrs. Wilson," she said, her voice stronger now.

"And in the meantime," I continued, "is there anything else I can do for you? Anything to make things a bit easier?"

She shook her head, managing a small smile. "The other members of the coven have been really good about making sure I'm fed and looked after," she said. "I'm okay, really."

I nodded, though I made a mental note to check in on her regularly. "All right, Isabella. But remember, you can call me anytime if you need anything, okay?"

She nodded, and with that, Meri and I said our goodbyes, leaving Isabella in the care of our coven family. As we walked away, I couldn't help but feel a pang of worry for the young witch. But for now, all we could do was continue our investigation and hope for the best.

Once Meri and I were back at home, we settled into the comfortable familiarity of the attic library. The journal that Isabella had given us lay on my desk, its pages filled with Isadora's neat handwriting. I hesitated for a moment, feeling a pang of guilt at the thought of reading someone else's private thoughts. But this was a matter of life and death, and we needed every piece of information we could get.

I opened the journal and began to read, Meri perched on the desk beside me. The entries were mostly businesslike, detailing Isadora's daily activities, her work at the library, and her interactions with the townsfolk. It was clear that she took her role as librarian seriously, and she was deeply committed to the library's success.

As I flipped through the pages, I came across an entry that stood out from the rest. Isadora's handwriting was more erratic, the words filled with emotion. She wrote about finding the skull, her family's heirloom, and the joy she felt at its discovery. But there was also a sense of unease. She seemed to believe that the theft of the skull was more than just a simple act of greed. There was a deeper meaning behind it, a significance that she couldn't quite grasp.

I read the passage over a few times, trying to glean any additional information from her words. But it was clear that Isadora herself didn't fully understand the situation. She was just as confused and concerned as we were.

"Well, Meri," I said, closing the journal and leaning back in my chair. "It seems we have more questions than answers."

Meri gave a noncommittal grunt, his eyes fixed on the journal. "That's usually how it goes, isn't it?"

I chuckled, despite the gravity of the situation. "Yes, I suppose it is."

I sat back in my chair, my eyes scanning over the journal entry once more. It was a simple note about Isadora tracing the heirloom to a local pawn shop, but something about it nagged at me. The more I thought about it, the more it seemed like there was something more to it, something potentially dangerous.

"Meri," I said, turning to my familiar, "I think Isadora might have gotten herself mixed up in something dangerous while she was looking for her heirloom."

Meri looked up from where he was lounging on the desk, his eyes meeting mine. "What makes you say that?"

I pointed to the journal entry. "This here. It didn't seem like much when I first read it, but now... I don't know. It just feels off."

Meri studied the entry for a moment before nodding. "I see what you mean. It's worth looking into, at least."

With the journal entry still echoing in my mind, I felt a renewed sense of purpose. I closed the journal gently, the worn leather cover warm under my fingers. I glanced at Meri, who was watching me with a curious expression.

"I think we need to show this to Thorn," I said, standing up and stretching my legs. Meri simply nodded, his gaze never leaving me.

As the evening rolled in, Thorn and I sat down for dinner. The food was delicious, but my mind was elsewhere. I kept glancing at the journal, which I had placed on the coffee table. Thorn noticed my distraction and raised an eyebrow in question.

"I found something in Isadora's journal," I said, deciding to get straight to the point. I got up and fetched the journal, flipping it open to the entry I had been pondering over.

I handed the journal to Thorn, watching as his eyes moved across the page, absorbing the words. There was a silence that stretched between us, filled only by the soft rustling of the journal pages under Thorn's fingers. He looked up, his gaze meeting mine, a thoughtful expression on his face.

"This is intriguing," he said, his voice carrying a note of determination. "We should definitely follow up on this."

I nodded, and Thorn continued, "I've been keeping an eye on Johnson since his peripheral involvement in the last murder case. Nothing solid has come up yet, but this... this could be a lead."

***

The town of Coventry was just beginning to stir as Thorn, Meri, and I made our way to Johnson's Pawn Shop. The shop was a recent addition to the town, housed in an old building just off the square. Its large display windows were filled with an assortment of items, from vintage jewelry to modern electronics, each one promising a bargain to the discerning buyer.

Upon entering the shop, the jingle of a bell announced our arrival. Behind the counter stood Fred Johnson, a man of advanced years with a lean frame and sharp, observant eyes. He glanced up at our entrance, his gaze briefly acknowledging Meri before returning to us.

"Thorn, Mrs. Wilson," he greeted in a gruff voice. "What brings you here this early?"

Thorn took the initiative, his tone professional. "We're investigating a matter involving Isadora," he began, watching Fred's reaction closely. "She mentioned that she traced a missing family heirloom to this pawn shop."

A frown creased Fred's forehead, his eyes darting between Thorn and me. "I don't recall any Isadora or any missing heirloom," he retorted defensively.

Not willing to let it go, I decided to press further. "Are you certain, Fred?" I asked, striving to keep my tone neutral. "Isadora was quite convinced that the heirloom had ended up here."

Fred's expression remained stubborn. "I've already told you, I don't know anything about it," he reiterated, his tone growing more irritable.

Despite his denials, I couldn't help but feel that Fred was withholding something. His evasiveness and defensive demeanor suggested he was hiding something.

As Thorn continued to press Fred with his questions, my attention was drawn away from their conversation. A faint, almost imperceptible shimmer on the floor near the backroom entrance caught my eye. To the untrained observer, it would have been easy to miss, but to someone attuned to the ebb and flow of magic, it was as clear as day. This was magical residue, and its presence here was both intriguing and concerning.

I quietly excused myself from Thorn and Fred's conversation, feigning a sudden interest in a dusty display case nearby. As I subtly moved closer to the shimmering spot, I could feel a faint hum of energy. It was a sensation I had come to associate with magic, and it was unmistakably present here.

I quickly rummaged through my purse, pulling out a tissue and an empty sandwich baggie that had previously held cheese crackers. With the tissue, I carefully swabbed the area, collecting a sample of the residue. I then placed the tissue in the baggie, sealing it carefully to ensure the sample remained undisturbed.

With the sample safely tucked away in my purse, I straightened up and looked back at the backroom entrance. The faint shimmer of magical residue was still there, a silent testament to the presence of magic in this seemingly mundane pawn shop. It was a discovery that raised more questions than it answered, and I couldn't help but feel a sense of apprehension. Magic, especially of the illicit kind, had no place in a pawn shop.

I made my way back to Thorn, who was concluding his conversation with Fred. The pawn shop owner's face was a mask of feigned innocence, but I could see the tension in his posture. As we stepped out of the pawn shop and into the bright morning light, I turned to Thorn, my voice barely above a whisper.

"I found something," I began, my words measured. "Magical residue, near the backroom. It's possible that Fred is dealing in more than just second-hand goods. He might be involved in the trade of stolen magical artifacts, maybe even the dangerous potion we found."

Thorn's brow furrowed in thought, his gaze distant as he considered the implications of my discovery. "If Isadora stumbled upon this," he mused, "it could provide a motive for her attack."

His gaze met mine, a serious look in his eyes. "We're dealing with something potentially dangerous here," he said, his tone grave. "We need to proceed with caution. If what you suspect is true, we're not just dealing with a simple assault case anymore."

Thorn and I exchanged a glance, our next steps clear in our minds. "I'm going to head back to the station," Thorn announced, his voice carrying a note of determination. "I need to secure a search warrant for this place. If there's any evidence here that could shed light on the attack on Isadora, we need to uncover it."

I nodded in agreement, my hand instinctively reaching for my purse where the sample of magical residue was safely tucked away. "I'll take this residue to Summoned Goods & Sundries," I said, meeting Thorn's gaze. "I should be able to identify what it is there. It could give us a clearer picture of what we're dealing with."

With our plan set, we parted ways. Thorn strode off towards his cruiser parked a short distance away, while Meri and I set off on foot. Summoned Goods & Sundries was just a short walk away.

After leaving Thorn, Meri and I made our way to the shop. It was a familiar place, filled with the scent of herbs and the quiet hum of magic. I went straight to the back room, where I had a workspace I could use for the purpose of identifying magical substances.

I carefully unsealed the sandwich baggie, the crinkling sound of the plastic echoing in the quiet room. I gently tipped the bag, allowing the sample of residue to spill out onto a clean, white piece of parchment. The substance was a fine powder, almost like dust, but it shimmered with a faint, otherworldly glow that was distinctly magical.

I leaned in, peering at the substance through an enchanted crystal magnifying glass. The magnification revealed a complex structure, a kaleidoscope of colors dancing within the tiny particles. It was beautiful, in a way, but also deeply mysterious.

I reached for a wand, a slender piece of hawthorn wood that had been in my family for generations. I began to chant a series of identification spells, each one designed to reveal the nature of a magical substance. But as I weaved the magic, I was met with resistance. The spells fizzled out, leaving the substance unchanged.

I tried again, using different spells, different incantations, but the result was the same. The substance remained a mystery, its secrets locked away. I had encountered many magical substances in my time, but this one was different. It was unlike anything I had ever seen before, and it was clear that I would need help to identify it.

I decided to seek help from someone with more experience in dealing with unusual magical substances. Lilith, with her vast knowledge and unconventional approach to magic, was the obvious choice.

I packed up the sample and left Summoned Goods & Sundries, Meri trotting along at my side. The sun was shifting in the sky, casting long shadows across the town square, and I refused to look up at the courthouse when we passed. The town was already alive with activity, the quiet of the early morning replaced by the bustling energy of Coventry's residents and visitors.

As we walked through the town square, we passed groups of tourists, their excited chatter filling the air.

Locals sat outside the cafes, sipping their morning coffee and enjoying the pleasant weather.

A few blocks over, Lilith's Victorian home came into view. I felt a familiar sense of trepidation as we approached. Lilith was a wealth of knowledge, but her insights often came with a side of discomfort.

We ascended the steps to Lilith's front door, the old wood creaking under our weight. I reached out and pressed the doorbell, its chime echoing through the house. We waited, the sounds of Coventry's morning activity fading into the background.

The door swung open, revealing Lilith. Her gray hair was pulled up into a loose bun, her sharp eyes assessing us.

"Back so soon?" she asked, her voice filled with amusement. "What can I do for you this time?"

"I found something," I said, reaching into my purse to pull out the sandwich baggie containing the magical residue. "At the pawn shop. I think it might be connected to what happened to Isadora."

Lilith's eyes narrowed as she took in the baggie, her expression turning serious. "Let's see what we can find out," she said, stepping aside to let us in.

Once inside, Lilith disappeared into her kitchen, reappearing moments later with a bottle of Coke for me. "You might need this," she said, handing me the bottle. "This could take a while."

With that, she beckoned Meri to follow her, leaving me alone in the parlor with my thoughts and my Coke. As they disappeared deeper into the house, I couldn't help but feel a sense of unease. Whatever the residue was, it was clear that it was linked to Isadora's attack. The question was, how?

Lilith had left me with a bottle of Coke, and I took a sip. I turned the mystery of the magical residue over in my mind, the unanswered questions forming a puzzle.

The wait seemed to stretch on, the silence of the parlor punctuated only by the distant murmur of Lilith's and Meri's voices and the occasional creak of the old house settling. Oh, and the odd colorful swear word… I found myself absently tracing the pattern on the armrest of the chair I was sitting in.

Finally, after what felt like an age, I heard the sound of approaching footsteps. I straightened in my chair, setting my now empty Coke bottle on the coffee table as Lilith and Meri reentered the room. Lilith's face was set in a serious expression, her eyes meeting mine with a gravity that instantly set me on edge.

"We've identified the residue," she said, her voice steady. She paused, as if gathering her thoughts, before continuing. "It's the same herb. The one I identified from the potion bottle."

The words hung in the air, heavy with implications. The residue, the potion, the attack on Isadora - they were all connected.

I stood from the plush armchair, the Coke bottle in my hand. "Lilith," I began, my voice carrying a note of gratitude. "I can't thank you enough for your help."

Lilith waved a dismissive hand at me, her eyes twinkling with a mischievous light. "Oh, don't mention it, dear. I do love a good mystery. Besides, it's not every day I get to flex my analytical muscles."

Meri, who had been unusually quiet, gave a soft chuff of amusement from his spot by the door. I shot him a look, but he merely swished his tail, his eyes gleaming with mirth.

"But," Lilith continued, her tone turning teasing, "next time you come asking for help, you could at least bring some donuts."

I laughed "Deal," I agreed. "Next time, donuts it is."

With that, Meri and I bid Lilith goodbye.

Halfway on our walk home, my phone buzzed, breaking through my thoughts. I pulled it out and saw a message from Thorn. He had secured a warrant for the pawn shop. It was a small victory, but a victory nonetheless.

I quickened my pace, Meri keeping up easily. We got home, and I immediately got in my car and headed back to the square.

Chapter Nine

As we approached, I spotted Thorn and Jeremy, another officer from the station, waiting outside the shop. Thorn was leaning against his cruiser, arms crossed over his chest, while Jeremy stood nearby, flipping through a small notebook. They both looked up as we approached, Thorn pushing off the cruiser to greet us.

"Hey," he nodded, a hint of a smile tugging at the corners of his mouth. "Meri."

"Thorn, Jeremy," I returned the greeting, glancing at the pawn shop. "Ready to get this search started?"

Thorn nodded. "We're all set. But," he added, his gaze thoughtful as he looked at the pawn shop, "we're not expecting to find much. We already know about Fred's hidden compartment in the basement, but he's probably too smart to keep anything there now that we know about it. He's likely moved anything of interest elsewhere."

Jeremy chimed in, closing his notebook and tucking it into his pocket, "Still, we have to check. You never know what we might find."

"All right, let's do this," Thorn said, glancing at me. "Remember, we're not sure what we'll find. Fred might have moved his stash."

I nodded, my gaze drifting to the pawn shop's front door. "I can't believe he's still using that hidden compartment. He has to know we're onto him."

Thorn shrugged, a wry smile tugging at the corners of his mouth. "Some people never learn."

With that, we approached the entrance. Thorn knocked on the door, warrant in hand. After a moment, the door creaked open, revealing Fred Johnson. His eyes widened slightly at the sight of the warrant, but he quickly composed himself and stepped aside to let us in.

Thorn and Jeremy moved with purpose, heading straight for the hidden basement compartment. I followed at a distance, my eyes scanning the shop. It was a hodgepodge of items, from vintage records to antique jewelry. But my focus was on the hidden compartment.

As Thorn opened it, I moved closer, my senses alert for any hint of magic. Inside the compartment were various items - electronics, unmarked bottles, and an assortment of other not-very-legal-looking stuff. But as I reached out with my magic, I felt nothing. No trace of the rare herb or any other magical substance.

I shook my head in disbelief, turning to Thorn. "Nothing magical," I reported, my voice filled with frustration. "I can't believe he's still using this compartment for illegal stuff, but nothing magical."

Thorn sighed, running a hand through his hair. "Well, we knew it was a long shot. We'll just have to keep looking."

Thorn and Jeremy were thorough in their search, methodically examining every corner of the pawn shop. I trailed behind them, my magical senses tingling as I scanned the room. The shop was a chaotic jumble of items, a hodgepodge of the ordinary and the unusual. Yet, amidst the disorder, a subtle pulse of magic drew my attention.

I traced the source of the magical pulse, my gaze landing on an unremarkable shelf. The pulse was stronger here, a clear indication of concealed magic. With a swift gesture, I invoked a basic detection spell. The shelf flickered under the spell's influence, revealing a hidden door.

"Thorn, Jeremy," I called, my voice echoing slightly in the quiet shop. "You might want to see this."

They quickly joined me, their expressions turning to surprise as they took in the sight of the hidden door. With Thorn's nod of approval, I pushed the door open, revealing a secret room that was a stark contrast

118

to the rest of the shop. We found meticulously organized shelves lined with jars of herbs and artifacts carefully displayed.

On a small desk, I found a ledger. Flipping it open, I found detailed records of transactions involving the buying and selling of illegal magical artifacts. In it, I found a recent entry for the same rare and expensive herb that was in the bottle found at the scene of Isadora's attack. The initials next to the entry were CH.

"Thorn," I said. "Look at this."

I handed him the ledger, pointing to the entry. His eyes narrowed as he read it, his expression hardening. "CH could be Charlie Hopper," he muttered, his voice filled with a mix of realization and frustration. "She was the one who tipped us off about Fred."

The connection was too blatant to ignore. But the question remained, what was Charlie's role in all of this?

With the discovery of the hidden room and the ledger, our next course of action was clear: we needed to find Charlie Hopper. Thorn pulled out his phone, dialing the number Charlie had given him. The call went to voicemail, and Thorn left a brief message asking her to return his call as soon as possible.

Meanwhile, Jeremy had already sprung into action. He decided to split off from us, intending to canvas the area where Charlie was last seen around the sheriff's station. Thorn and I, on the other hand, decided to follow a different lead.

Our first stop was the local diner, a bustling hub of activity where locals gathered for their daily dose of gossip and comfort food. The owner, a friendly woman named Betty, greeted us warmly but couldn't recall seeing Charlie recently.

Undeterred, we moved on to the local hardware store, a place where newcomers often stopped by for supplies to settle into their new homes. The store owner, a gruff man named Hank, recognized Charlie from our description but hadn't seen her in a few days.

Our search took us to various other businesses around town, but no one seemed to have any recent information about Charlie. The day was wearing on, and our leads were dwindling. We decided to make one last stop at Craft Donuts, my own donut shop, before calling it a day.

Chalfy was behind the counter, serving a fresh batch of glazed donuts to the only customer ahead of us. He greeted us with a broad smile and a couple of donuts on the house. As we munched on the donuts at the counter, we explained our predicament.

Chalfy's face lit up with recognition when we mentioned Charlie. "Oh, I remember her! She came in here a few times. Nice lady, seemed a bit quiet though," he said. When we asked if he knew where we could find her, he suggested, "You know, Marianne might be able to help. She's the real estate agent who helps folks find rentals in town."

"Ah, Marianne! Why didn't I think of her?" I exclaimed, slapping my forehead lightly. Thorn chuckled at my theatrics, but I could see the spark of hope in his eyes.

We made our way to Marianne's office, a charming little building nestled between a dentist and a florist. The office was cozy and inviting, with pictures of various properties adorning the walls and a small coffee table laden with real estate magazines. The scent of fresh coffee wafted through the air, adding to the welcoming atmosphere.

"Marianne, we're hoping you can help us," Thorn began, explaining our search for Charlie. Marianne's eyes widened in recognition as we described Charlie.

"Oh, yes, I remember Charlie," she said, her fingers tapping on her desk as she thought. "Quiet woman, kept to herself mostly. I did help her find a rental property."

She rummaged through her drawers, pulling out a file. "Here we are," she said, handing us a piece of paper with an address written on it. "This is where I helped her find a place."

We thanked Marianne for her help, the address in hand providing a solid lead in our search for Charlie. Thorn and I made our way to the rental property. It was a modest two-story house, nestled in a quiet neighborhood. We were so close to finding Charlie, I could almost taste it. And I had convinced myself that she was the end of the case.

Thorn and I arrived at the rental property, a quaint two-story house nestled in a quiet neighborhood. The front yard was well-kept, and the house itself had a welcoming aura. Thorn led the way to the front door, knocking firmly. After a few moments, the door swung open.

"Charlie Hopper," Thorn began, his tone professional yet cordial. "We have a few more questions for you."

The woman blinked, looking taken aback. "Oh, I think there's been a misunderstanding," she said, her voice soft. "I'm Christine. Charlie's my twin sister."

Chapter Ten

"May we come in and speak with you?" Thorn asked, his tone carrying the weight of his position but maintaining a polite edge. Christine, taken aback, hesitated for a moment before stepping aside and gesturing for us to enter.

"Of course, please come in," she said, leading us through the front door.

The interior of the house had the worn-in feel of a rental property. The walls were painted a neutral beige, the carpet beneath our feet was a little threadbare, and the furniture had seen better days. Yet, there was a certain charm to it, a testament to the lives lived within its walls.

Christine led us to the kitchen, a functional space that had seen its fair share of use. The cabinets were a faded wood, the countertops were a scratched laminate, and the linoleum floor was slightly discolored in high-traffic areas. A sturdy table, surrounded by a mismatched set of chairs, sat in the middle of the room, a beacon of homeyness in the otherwise utilitarian space.

As we took our seats, Christine busied herself with making coffee. The aroma filled the room, a comforting scent that seemed to soften the edges of the worn kitchen. To my surprise, she even retrieved a can of oysters from a cupboard and gave it to Meri, who accepted it with a pleased chirp.

Once the coffee was ready, Christine joined us at the table, her expression serious. "All right," she said, her gaze moving between Thorn and me. "What can I help you with?"

Thorn cleared his throat, his gaze steady on Christine. "We're here because we're investigating a smuggling ring and a recent attack on a local woman named Isadora," he began, his voice carrying the weight of his position.

Christine's brows furrowed at the mention of the smuggling ring, her hands tightening around her coffee mug. "Smuggling ring?" she echoed, her voice barely above a whisper.

Thorn nodded, continuing with the details of our investigation. He mentioned the pawn shop, the stolen magical artifacts, the dangerous herb, and the connection we had found to her sister, Charlie.

With each revelation, Christine's expression grew increasingly troubled. Her eyes widened, her mouth opened and closed a few times as if she wanted to interrupt, but she remained silent, letting Thorn finish.

When Thorn finally concluded, the room fell into a heavy silence. Christine seemed to be processing the information, her gaze distant. Then, she shook her head, a look of disbelief etched on her face.

"I... I can't believe this," she stammered, her voice shaky. "Charlie... involved in something like this? It's... it's impossible. She's out of town, but... but she wouldn't... she couldn't be involved in something like this."

Her words were filled with conviction, but there was a hint of uncertainty in her eyes. It was clear that our visit had shaken her, and she was struggling to come up with something to say.

As Christine continued to express her disbelief, my gaze drifted to the necklace she was wearing. It was a simple chain, but the pendant caught my attention. It was a small, intricately carved stone, glowing with a faint, ethereal light. It was the kind of light that I recognized as magical.

I glanced at Thorn, who was also eyeing the necklace. I could see the recognition in his eyes. We had both seen the description of a similar necklace in the ledger from Fred's pawn shop. It was listed as one of the stolen magical artifacts.

"Christine," I began, my voice gentle, "where did you get that necklace?"

She looked down, her fingers instinctively reaching for the pendant. "This?" she asked, looking back up at us. "Charlie gave it to me. She said she found it at a flea market. Why?"

Thorn and I exchanged a glance. It was becoming increasingly clear that Charlie's involvement in this was deeper than we had initially thought. And now, her twin sister was unknowingly wearing evidence around her neck.

"Excuse me," I interjected, as Thorn continued his conversation with Christine. "Could I use your restroom?"

Christine looked surprised for a moment, but quickly recovered. "Of course," she said, pointing towards the staircase. "The guest bathroom is upstairs, first door on the left."

"Thank you," I replied, standing up and making my way towards the stairs. As I ascended, I could hear the muffled voices of Thorn and Christine continuing their conversation below.

Reaching the top of the stairs, I paused. Instead of turning left towards the bathroom, I turned right, my gaze falling on the door of the only bedroom that appeared to be in use. The other two rooms were either empty or looked to be being used for storage. I hesitated for a moment, then pushed the door open and stepped inside.

The bedroom was simply decorated, with a double bed pushed against one wall and a wooden dresser standing tall on the other. The room was impeccably neat, the bed made with military precision and not a single item out of place. It gave the impression of being inhabited by a single person, a meticulous one at that.

I began my search with a systematic approach, starting with the bed. I crouched down, my eyes scanning the space beneath the bed frame. It was clean and empty, not even a speck of dust to be seen. Next, I moved to the mattress, lifting it with care, but it too held no secrets.

Feeling a twinge of disappointment, I turned my attention to the closet. I opened the door, my fingers sifting through the hanging clothes, but found nothing unusual. The floor of the closet was just as ordinary, with a pair of shoes neatly lined up against the wall.

With a sigh, I moved to the last place left to search - the wooden dresser. I pulled open the top drawer, revealing a collection of neatly folded clothes. However, it was a small box tucked away in the corner that caught my attention. I opened the box and was met with two sets of identification. The photos on both IDs were identical, but the names were different - one read Charlie Hopper, and the other, Christine Hopper.

A shiver of realization ran through me. The twins had been living a dual life, swapping identities as needed. I quickly pulled out my phone, capturing a picture of the IDs. With a final glance around the room, I carefully replaced the box in its original position, ensuring everything was as I had found it. The implications of this discovery were significant, and I knew I had to share this with Thorn as soon as possible. But for now, I had to maintain my composure and act as if everything was normal.

I was so engrossed in my search that I didn't hear the soft footsteps ascending the stairs. It wasn't until the bedroom door swung open with a suddenness that made me jump that I realized I wasn't alone. Christine stood in the doorway, her eyes wide with shock and suspicion. Her gaze darted from me to the open dresser drawer and back again.

"What are you doing in here?" she demanded, her voice sharp. Her eyes were hard, her posture rigid with tension.

I straightened up slowly, meeting her gaze without flinching. I had been caught, but I wasn't about to back down. "Christine," I began, keeping my voice steady despite the adrenaline coursing through my veins. "I found something interesting in your dresser."

Her eyes flickered to the dresser and then back to me. I could see the panic starting to creep into her expression, but she was doing her best to keep it under control. "What... what are you talking about?" she stammered, her voice betraying her fear.

I pulled out my phone, showing her the picture of the IDs. "These," I said, my voice calm but firm. "Two IDs, same picture, different names. If these were legitimate, they wouldn't have the exact same picture. You and Charlie are up to something, aren't you?"

Christine's eyes darted between me and the picture on my phone, her face growing paler by the second. She opened her mouth to speak, then closed it again, her gaze dropping to the floor. She seemed to be grappling with herself, torn between maintaining her facade and confessing the truth.

"No," she finally said, her voice barely more than a whisper. "That's not... I mean, it's not what you think."

She moved to sit on the edge of the bed, her hands wringing together in her lap. I watched her, waiting patiently for her to continue. She took a deep breath, her shoulders rising and falling with the effort.

"Charlie... Charlie isn't real," she admitted, her voice shaky. "She's... she's me. I use her as an alias sometimes." She had been living a double life, using her fabricated twin sister as a cover.

The sound of footsteps on the stairs announced Thorn's arrival. He appeared in the doorway, his brows furrowing as he took in the scene before him. I quickly filled him in on Christine's confession, watching as his expression hardened.

Christine, for her part, didn't shy away from Thorn's scrutiny. She met his gaze head-on, her own eyes filled with a mix of defiance and fear. When Thorn asked her about her involvement in the smuggling ring, she nodded.

"Yes, I was involved," she admitted, her voice steady. "But I didn't have anything to do with the attack on Isadora. I swear." Christine's gaze dropped to her hands, which were clasped tightly in her lap. "I didn't want to get involved," she began, her voice barely above a whisper. "But my ex-boyfriend... he was the one who started all this. He's the one running the smuggling ring."

Thorn leaned forward, his eyes narrowing. "What's his name, Christine?" he asked, his voice firm.

Christine's eyes darted up to meet Thorn's, a flicker of fear passing through them. "I... I can't," she stammered, her voice trembling. "I can't tell you his name."

"Why not?" Thorn pressed, his tone softening slightly. "Christine, we can help you. But we need his name."

But Christine shook her head, her lips pressed into a thin line. "No," she said, her voice barely audible. "I can't. I just can't." The fear in her eyes was palpable, and it was clear that whatever hold her ex-boyfriend had over her, it was strong enough to keep her silent.

Thorn's expression was stern as he leaned against the doorframe, crossing his arms over his chest. "Christine, if you don't give us someone else to arrest for these crimes, I'm going to have no choice but to lock you up."

Despite his words, Christine remained stubbornly silent. It was clear that she was terrified of her ex-boyfriend, and that fear was stronger than her fear of going to jail.

With a heavy sigh, Thorn stood up from the table, his expression stern. "Christine," he began, his voice carrying a note of regret, "I'm afraid I have to place you under arrest."

Christine's eyes widened, but she didn't protest. She seemed to have been expecting this outcome. Thorn gently but firmly guided her to her feet, reciting her rights as he handcuffed her.

"I'm sorry, Christine," he said, his voice soft. "But we have enough evidence to charge you with several crimes. We'll have to hold you in custody until we can sort this out."

Christine nodded, her face pale but resigned. As Thorn led her out of the house, I couldn't help but feel a pang of sympathy for her. She was clearly in over her head, caught up in a dangerous situation she didn't fully understand. But for now, our priority had to be finding the person who hurt Isadora.

***

As Thorn drove away with Christine in the back of his squad car, Meri and I were left standing on the sidewalk. "We need to figure out our next move," I said.

"We could go back to the lake," he suggested, his voice low. "There might be something we missed the first time."

"You're right," I agreed, nodding decisively. "Mostly because I can't think of anything else right now..."

"I'm a genius."

"Sure."

"Whatever."

Meri and I returned to the lake where the attack on Isadora had taken place. We walked along the water's edge, the gentle lapping of the waves against the shore a stark contrast to the violence that had occurred here. I could feel the faint hum of magic in the air, a residual echo of the powerful spell that had been cast. It was like a whisper on the wind, a ghostly reminder of the attack.

I knelt down, my fingers brushing against the cool earth as I focused my senses. There was a faint trace of something, a residue that was almost invisible to the naked eye. I was confident that it was the same herb that Lilith had identified in the potion bottle and at Fred's pawn shop. Carefully, I collected a sample just in case. I had been wrong before.

I rose to my feet, dusting off my jeans as I turned to Meri. His eyes were on me, waiting for me to share what I'd found.

"Meri, I think the attacker used the potion to enhance their magic during the attack on Isadora."

Meri's ears perked up at this, his gaze intense as he processed my words. I continued, "It's similar to what Isadora had planned for the fireworks display. She wanted to use a potion to boost her fire power."

"We're dealing with someone who knew exactly what they were doing,"

Meri began laughing hysterically.

"What?"

"Well, I mean… duh. That's not exactly a huge breakthrough, Kinsley. We are making exactly zero progress, and I'm hungry."

"I'm hungry too," I admitted. "Let's get some donuts and go see Lilith to confirm this potion is what I think it is."

"I want bacon."

"We have bacon at Craft Donuts for the maple bacon donuts."

"Fine."

"Fine."

"Whatever."

Chapter Eleven

With a fresh lead and a dozen donuts from Craft Donuts in hand, Meri and I made our way back to Lilith's house. We needed Lilith's expertise, and I hoped the donuts would serve as a small token of our appreciation. I felt kind of bad that we just kept showing up to ask for help.

The door swung open to reveal Lilith, her eyes immediately darting to the box of pastries with a spark of delight. "Ah, you've come bearing gifts this time," she said, a playful smile tugging at the corners of her mouth. "I suppose I can't turn you away now, can I?"

We shared a laugh as she ushered us into her home, her eyes lingering on the box of donuts with undisguised anticipation. Once we were settled in her parlor, I carefully opened the box, revealing the colorful array of pastries. Lilith's eyes widened in delight, and she quickly selected a donut, taking a bite with a satisfied hum.

After a few moments of enjoying our treats, I decided it was time to get down to business. I reached into my bag and pulled out the sandwich baggie containing the magical residue we had found at the lake. I handed it to Lilith, watching as her expression shifted from relaxed to focused.

"I was hoping you could help us identify this," I said, gesturing to the baggie. "We found it at the lake where the attack happened."

Lilith nodded, her gaze fixed on the baggie. "Of course, I'd be happy to help," she said, her tone serious. "Why don't you come with me? You can watch as I work this time."

"Really?"

"Well, if I don't teach you, you're going to keep showing up and asking me to do it for you…"

"I'm sorry."

"Don't apologize," she said with a laugh. "It's always good to see you, and I do love donuts. But I should teach you."

"Thank you."

Lilith led the way into her dining room, a space that had been repurposed into a magical workspace. The large wooden table, usually the centerpiece for family meals and gatherings, was now a hub of mystical activity. A mini cauldron, its surface dark and gleaming, sat in the middle, surrounded by an array of magical tools and ingredients.

"Let's get to work," Lilith said, her tone businesslike as she moved to the table. She carefully transferred a small amount of the residue from the baggie into the cauldron. I watched, fascinated, as she began to add various ingredients, each one carefully measured and meticulously added.

"The first step is to introduce the sample to a neutral medium," she explained. "This allows us to break down the potion into its base components without altering their properties."

Next, she reached for a small vial filled with a clear liquid. "This is distilled moonwater," she said, pouring a measured amount into the cauldron. "It helps to amplify the magical properties of the potion, making it easier to identify each ingredient."

As the moonwater mixed with the residue, the mixture in the cauldron began to shimmer with a soft, ethereal light. Lilith watched this with a keen eye, her fingers tracing symbols in the air above the cauldron. "Now, we wait for the potion to react. Each potion has a unique reaction to moonwater. The color, the smell, the intensity of the light... all these can give us clues about the nature of the potion."

She then turned her attention to a collection of small jars, each filled with a different herb or ingredient. "While we wait for the reaction, we can start identifying the individual components. The residue you brought has a distinct smell, a combination of the different ingredients used in the potion. By comparing this smell to the ones in these jars, we can start to identify the ingredients."

The process was meticulous and time-consuming, but I found myself captivated by it. Watching Lilith work was like watching a master artist at work, each movement precise and purposeful. And through it all, I could see the deep respect she had for the craft, a respect that I shared.

Finally, after what felt like hours, Lilith straightened up, a thoughtful expression on her face. "This is a potent potion," she said, her voice serious. "It's designed to enhance a witch's power, making them virtually unstoppable for a short time. But it's also incredibly dangerous. The user risks their life every time they use it."

The attacker had used this potion to enhance their power, not caring about the potential cost to their own life.

"I don't like being a snitch," she began, her voice low, "but there's someone in Coventry who might be involved in this. His name is Li Shu."

She paused, her gaze steady on mine. "He's a dealer in illicit potions and herbs. Black market stuff. He won't deal with members of our coven, but I've heard of him through... well, let's just call them my 'contacts.'"

The name didn't ring any bells for me, but the way Lilith spoke of him suggested he was someone to be wary of. "Do you think he could have supplied the potion to the attacker?" I asked.

Lilith shrugged, a grimace pulling at her lips. "It's possible. He's known for dealing in the rare and dangerous. If anyone in Coventry could get their hands on that herb, it would be him."

The information was a lead, albeit a potentially dangerous one. But if it brought us closer to finding Isadora's attacker, it was a risk I was willing to take.

"Thank you for your help."

"Do you want me to come with you to talk to Li?" Lilith asked a little too enthusiastically.

"No, I'm going to run all this info by Thorn. He'll want to go."

"Boo. You're no fun, but thanks for the donuts."

"You're welcome…"

"Anyway, here's Li's address. His shop is in his basement. You'll need a password that he changes daily. My contacts tell me it's written in magical ink on the bottom left of his doorframe. He won't want to talk to you, but he is afraid of our coven shutting down his little side business. So, you should be able to intimidate him into spilling his guts. Oh, and blow a little of this in his face." Lilith handed me a tiny baggy filled with dark powder. "Just a pinch will do the trick."

"What is this?"

"Better you don't know."

***

As Meri and I left Lilith's house, I felt a sense of urgency mixed with a strange calm. We had a new lead, a name that could potentially bring us closer to finding the person responsible for Isadora's attack. The name Li Shu was now etched in my mind, a dealer in illicit potions and herbs, operating in the shadows of Coventry's magical community.

We got into the car, Meri hopping into the passenger seat with his usual enthusiasm. As I started the motor, I glanced at him, his intelligent eyes meeting mine. He seemed to understand the gravity of the situation, his usual playful demeanor replaced with a more serious one.

The drive to the sheriff's station was a quiet one. The streets of Coventry were bustling with activity, people going about their day, oblivious to the dark undercurrents running beneath the surface of our town. The contrast was stark, and it served as a reminder of the dual life I led, straddling the mundane and the magical.

As we pulled up to the sheriff's station, I took a moment to gather my thoughts. Thorn was not just my husband, but also the sheriff, and he had a right to know about the dangerous elements operating in our town. But I also knew that this information would pull him deeper into the magical world, a world that could be dangerous for those unprepared.

Stepping out of the car, I took a deep breath, steeling myself for the conversation ahead. Meri and I walked into the station, the familiar surroundings offering a sense of comfort. Thorn was at his desk, engrossed in some paperwork. As he looked up and saw us, his face broke into a warm smile. I returned the smile, feeling a surge of gratitude for his unwavering support.

Taking a seat across from him, I prepared to share what we had discovered, hoping that this new lead would bring us closer to finding Isadora's attacker.

"Thorn," I began, my voice steady despite the gravity of the information I was about to share. "We've made some progress in the investigation."

His eyebrows lifted in interest, his pen pausing over the paperwork he'd been working on. "Oh?"

I nodded, taking a deep breath before launching into the details. "Meri and I went back to the lake where Isadora was attacked. We found more of the magical residue there, the same kind that was in the potion bottle and at Fred's pawn shop."

Thorn's expression grew serious as he took in this information. "And you're sure it's the same substance?"

"I'm certain," I confirmed. "I took a sample and brought it to Lilith. She confirmed it was the same rare herb she identified from the potion bottle."

Thorn leaned back in his chair, his gaze thoughtful as he processed this. "So, the attacker used this potion to enhance their magic during the attack on Isadora?"

"That's what we believe," I said. "And there's more. Lilith gave us a lead on a possible suspect."

Thorn's eyes narrowed slightly. "Who?"

"A man named Li Shu," I replied. "He's a dealer in illicit potions and herbs. Lilith knows of him through her... contacts. He operates in the black market, and he doesn't deal with members of our coven."

Thorn was silent for a moment, his gaze distant as he considered this new information. "This could be the break we need," he finally said, his voice filled with determination. "We need to find this Li Shu."

"Actually," I interjected, a small smile playing on my lips, "we might be a step ahead on that front."

Thorn looked at me, curiosity piqued. "Oh?"

I nodded, reaching into my bag to pull out a small piece of paper. Unfolding it, I slid it across the desk towards him. "Lilith gave me an address. She believes this is where we can find Li Shu."

Thorn picked up the paper, his eyes scanning the address. A slow, determined smile spread across his face. "Well, then," he said, standing up from his desk and grabbing his jacket, "let's not waste any time. We have a potion dealer to question."

***

The address Lilith had given us led to a nondescript suburban house, the kind of place you'd drive past without a second glance. Thorn and I approached the front door. I knocked, and after a moment, the door creaked open just a crack. A pair of wary eyes peered out at us.

"We're here to see Li Shu," I said, trying to keep my voice steady. The eyes narrowed suspiciously, and the door started to close. Thinking quickly, I blurted out the code word I'd interpreted from the door frame. It had been right where Lilith had said it would be.

Fortunately, it seemed the Li didn't recognize me on sight. Probably because I'd never seen or heard of him before. A testament to how adeptly he avoided members of my family.

Li Shu led us through the house and down a set of stairs into a basement. The basement was dimly lit, filled with shelves of jars and bottles containing all manner of strange and exotic ingredients. Li Shu stood behind a makeshift counter, watching us warily.

Thorn, standing tall and authoritative, took a step forward, his gaze never leaving Li Shu. "We're investigating an attack on a local witch," he began, his voice steady and firm. "During our investigation, we found a potion at the scene of the crime. A potion containing a rare herb."

Li Shu's eyes flickered at the mention of the herb, but he quickly regained his composure. "I don't know what you're talking about," he said, his voice steady, but his eyes darting between Thorn and me.

Thorn continued, undeterred by Li's denial. "This isn't a common herb, Li," he said, his tone stern. "It's rare, and it's expensive. And we have reason to believe it came from here."

Li Shu's eyes widened slightly, but he quickly shook his head. "I don't deal in rare herbs," he said, his voice firm. "I don't know anything about this."

Thorn's gaze didn't waver. "We're not accusing you of anything, Li," he said calmly. "We're just trying to find out who might have bought this herb from you."

Li Shu's gaze flickered between Thorn and me, his expression unreadable. After a moment, he sighed. "I can't help you," he said, his voice barely above a whisper. "I don't keep records of my customers."

I watched him carefully, my hand dipping into my pocket to retrieve the small baggie of powder Lilith had given me. As Thorn continued to press Li, I opened the baggie, the fine powder glinting under the dim basement lights. With a swift motion, I blew a small cloud of the powder towards Li Shu.

The moment the powder met the air, a subtle shift occurred in Li Shu. His eyes, previously narrowed in defiance, widened in surprise. He blinked rapidly, the powder settling on his face, and his gaze shifted from Thorn to me. It was as if he was seeing me for the first time.

His defensive posture slackened, his arms dropping to his sides. His eyes, now wide and alert, were locked onto the baggie in my hand. The powder, a magical truth serum of sorts, had its intended effect. The denial that had been so readily on his lips moments ago was replaced by a reluctant admission.

"People have been asking for it," he confessed, his voice barely above a whisper. His eyes flickered between Thorn and me, a newfound wariness in his gaze. Li's gaze dropped to the floor, his fingers drumming nervously on the armrest of his chair.

"There is a potion," he began, his voice barely above a whisper. "It's highly sought after by a certain group of... individuals. They practice dark magic, and they live around Coventry, but they keep to themselves. The town prefers it that way, and so do they."

He paused, taking a deep breath before continuing. "I've had several people come to my shop over the years, asking for this potion. But I've always turned them away. I don't carry it, and I don't sell it."

His words hung in the air, and I exchanged a glance with Thorn. I wasn't entirely convinced by Li's claims, but I also knew that pressing him further at this point would likely be fruitless. I could threaten him with punishment from my coven, but I didn't want to play that hand yet.

Thorn seemed to share my thoughts. He gave a curt nod. "All right, Li," he said, his voice firm. "We'll let this matter rest for now. But if we find out you've been lying to us, there will be consequences."

Li nodded, his face a mask of neutrality, but I could see the flicker of unease in his eyes. "I understand."

"Thank you for your time, Li," I said, my voice steady despite the whirlwind of thoughts in my head. He merely nodded in response, his gaze following us as we made our way towards the basement steps.

Before we could fully step away, Thorn turned back to him, a question lingering on his lips. "Li," he began, his voice steady, "where can we find these dark magic users you mentioned?"

Li paused, his gaze flickering between Thorn and me. He seemed to weigh his options, his lips pressed into a thin line. After a moment, he sighed, his shoulders slumping slightly. "They live in an old camp, outside of Coventry," he admitted.

Thorn's eyebrows shot up in surprise, but he quickly masked his reaction, maintaining his composed demeanor. "Can you give us directions?" he asked, his tone nonchalant.

Li hesitated, his gaze darting to the side. "It's not a place you can just find," he said, his voice laced with a hint of warning. "It's hidden, secluded. You'd need to know where to look."

"But you know," I interjected, my voice firm. Li's gaze snapped to me, his eyes wide. After a moment, he nodded, a resigned sigh escaping his lips.

He proceeded to give us vague directions, describing a winding path that led through the woods, past an old oak tree with a hollowed-out trunk, and towards a clearing where the camp was supposedly located. His instructions were cryptic, filled with landmarks rather than clear paths, but it was a start. With a final nod of thanks, Thorn and I left Li's house.

The revelations from our conversation with Li had only served to deepen the mystery surrounding Isadora's attack. The existence of a group of dark magic users in Coventry, the demand for a dangerous potion, Li's potential involvement - it was a tangled web that we were only just beginning to unravel.

As we settled back into the car, Thorn broke the silence. "You know," he began, his voice thoughtful, "I think I might have a vague idea of where this camp might be. I've heard rumors, whispers really, about an old camp outside of town."

His words sparked a memory in me, a story I'd heard when I was a kid. "Wait," I said, turning to look at him. "I remember hearing stories about an old abandoned camp too. Something about the county tearing out the road to keep teenagers from going there and partying."

Thorn's eyes met mine, a spark of recognition in his gaze. "Yes, that's it," he said, nodding. "I remember hearing the same thing. It's not easy to get to, we'll have to take a dirt road, but I think I can get us there."

Thorn expertly navigated the car down a narrow, winding dirt road that cut through the dense forest surrounding the town. The road was uneven and rough, and the car jostled us around as we ventured deeper into the woods. The only sounds that filled the silence were the crunch of small branches under the tires and the occasional call of a bird from the treetops. The atmosphere was thick with anticipation, the forest around us seeming to hold its breath as we ventured further away from the familiarity of Coventry.

After a considerable amount of time, the dense wall of trees began to thin out, revealing the entrance to what appeared to be an old summer camp. The sign that marked the entrance was weathered and faded, the paint chipped and worn from years of exposure to the elements. But beyond the sign, the buildings of the camp were surprisingly well-maintained. They stood in stark contrast to the wildness of the forest that surrounded them, a small pocket of civilization in the midst of nature.

As we pulled up to the entrance of the camp, a figure emerged from the closest building. He was tall, with a lean build that suggested a life of physical activity. His movements were fluid and deliberate, each step taken with a predator's grace. His features were sharp, his eyes keen and watchful, but his smile was polite. His voice was smooth as he introduced himself to us as soon as we were out of the car.

"Good afternoon," he greeted, his voice carrying a hint of amusement. "I'm Raven. I run this place."

Raven's demeanor was a study in contrasts. His polite smile and smooth voice were at odds with the predatory grace of his movements and the sharpness of his gaze. It was as if he was wearing a mask of civility, a thin veneer that did little to hide the sense of danger that seemed to radiate from him. It was disconcerting, to say the least, and my instincts were screaming at me to tread carefully.

Yet, despite the warning bells ringing in my head, Raven was nothing but cooperative. He didn't invite us into the camp, his polite smile never wavering as he explained, "I'm afraid I can't let you in without a warrant. Rules are rules, after all." But he made no move to dismiss us either, standing at the entrance and indicating with a sweep of his hand that he was willing to talk to us right there.

Thorn, ever the professional, didn't waste any time on pleasantries. His gaze was steady, his voice firm as he launched straight into the reason for our visit. "We're here as part of an investigation," he began, his tone leaving no room for misunderstanding. "There's been an attack in town on a woman named Isadora. You might have heard about it."

Raven's polite smile didn't waver, but there was a flicker of something in his eyes. Interest? Concern? It was hard to tell. "Yes, I've heard about it," he replied, his voice as smooth as ever. "A terrible thing."

Thorn nodded, his expression serious. "We believe a certain potion might have been involved in the attack," he continued, watching Raven closely for any signs of recognition or surprise. "A potion that enhances a witch's power, but can be deadly if misused."

Raven's polite smile didn't waver, but his eyes hardened slightly. "I can assure you, we had nothing to do with any attack," he said firmly. "On the night you're referring to, my group and I were at the town picnic. We kept to ourselves, but we were there. Your familiar even walked past us."

I glanced down at Meri, who was sitting attentively at my feet. His eyes met mine, and then he turned his gaze to study Raven. His eyes narrowed slightly as he took in the man's features, his head tilting in that thoughtful way of his.

"Meri," I began, keeping my voice low so only he could hear, "do you remember seeing this man and his group at the picnic?"

Meri's gaze remained fixed on Raven for a moment longer before he turned back to me. "Yes," he groused. "I remember him. He was there, with others. We're wasting our time again."

His confirmation solidified Raven's alibi in my mind. I looked back up at Raven, my gaze steady. "My familiar, Meri, confirms your alibi," I said, my voice carrying a note of reluctant acceptance. "He saw you and your group at the picnic."

Despite the unease that Raven's presence stirred within me, it seemed that he couldn't have been involved in the attack on Isadora. But that didn't mean he was entirely innocent. The question of the potion still remained.

With the question of Raven's alibi settled, I decided to press on the matter of the potion. "What about the potion?" I asked, my gaze steady on his face. "Do you know anything about it?"

Raven seemed to ignore the question, his gaze drifting off to the side as if lost in thought. After a moment, he turned his attention back to us. "You know, there's someone else you might want to look into," he said, his tone casual, as if he was merely suggesting a new restaurant rather than pointing us towards a potential suspect.

"Euna Welsh," he continued, his eyes meeting mine. "She used to be a mediocre witch, at best. But recently, I saw her planting an entire acre of her garden with a single spell. Given her skill level, that's... unlikely."

He paused, as if considering his next words. "Our properties are near each other, and I walk by her place often. We're on amicable enough terms. But that display of power... it was surprising, to say the least."

Euna Welsh, a mediocre witch suddenly displaying a significant increase in power? It was certainly worth looking into.

With our conversation concluded, Thorn and I made to leave. But before we could step away, I turned back to Raven, a stern look on my face. "If you and your witches are going to continue your ways, you should stay out of Coventry," I warned him.

Raven simply nodded, his expression unreadable. "We would never consider breaking the truce between our people and your town," he said, his voice calm and steady. I had no idea what truce he was referring to, but I decided to let it go for now.

"But you should reconsider your use of illicit potions," I added, my tone firm. "Before one of you gets hurt."

Raven shrugged, a nonchalant gesture that felt at odds with the intensity of his gaze. "I don't know what you're talking about," he said, but his eyes, dark and swirling with an undercurrent of violence, told a different story.

I nodded, deciding it was time to leave. "Let's go, Thorn," I said, and we turned to leave. As we drove away from the camp, I couldn't shake off the feeling of unease that Raven had instilled in me.

We didn't drive far before we reached a farm that we had passed on our way to the camp. After our conversation with Raven, we assumed it was Euna's place. We pulled over, ready to continue our investigation.

As Thorn parked the car along the gravel path, we took a moment to survey the property. The farmhouse was a charming structure, nestled amidst a sprawling garden that was proof of the owner's green thumb. Rows of vegetables and herbs were arranged with meticulous care, the plants thriving under the warm sun. A woman, presumably Euna, was bent over one of the rows, her hands busy with the task of weeding.

We exited the car, our shoes crunching on the gravel as we made our way towards her. As we neared, she straightened from her task, turning to face us. Her initial look of surprise quickly morphed into a guarded expression as she took in our presence. Thorn took the lead, introducing us and explaining our purpose for the visit.

Euna's response was swift and firm. "I don't know what you're talking about," she stated, her voice steady despite the accusation. "I think it's best if you leave."

Without waiting for a response, she turned away from us, striding towards a small garden shed situated at the edge of the property. We watched her retreating figure, and her denial did little to quell our suspicions

As we began to retreat from the property, a voice rang out, halting us in our tracks. "Wait!" it called, and we turned to see an elderly woman making her way towards us from the direction of the farmhouse. She moved with a slow, steady gait, her face etched with the lines of age but her eyes sparkling with a sharp, alert intelligence.

"Ethyl," she introduced herself as she drew nearer, extending a hand in greeting. "Ethyl Welsh. Euna's my daughter."

We exchanged introductions, and Ethyl gestured towards the porch of the farmhouse. "Why don't we sit a spell?" she suggested, and we followed her to a set of worn, but comfortable-looking, chairs.

As we settled in, Ethyl began to speak. "I couldn't help overhearing your conversation with Euna," she said, her gaze steady on Thorn. "You're looking into that attack on the young witch, aren't you?"

Thorn nodded, confirming her suspicion. "We are," he said. "We have reason to believe that a certain potion might have been involved."

Ethyl hummed thoughtfully, her gaze distant. "Well, if it's potions you're interested in, you might want to look into that charity Euna's been volunteering for," she said, her voice dropping to a conspiratorial whisper.

She went on to explain about At the Roots, a charity that claimed to be devoted to finding and supporting magical users living among humans, helping them discover their heritage. But Ethyl had her doubts about the organization.

"I used to volunteer there too," she admitted. "But I left after I started getting suspicious. Euna, though, she's still there."

Ethyl leaned forward in her chair, her hands clasped tightly around her mug as she began to recount her experience. "It was a few months back," she started, her voice dropping to a near whisper. "I was helping out at one of their events. I needed to find a restroom and ended up in a part of the building I hadn't been in before."

She paused, her gaze distant as she recalled the memory. "I stumbled upon a room," she continued, her voice steady despite the gravity of her words. "It was filled with all sorts of equipment, vials, herbs... it looked like a potion-making operation."

Her words hung heavy in the air, the implications clear. But before we could interject, she pressed on. "Before I could get a good look, Dori Messel, the witch who runs At the Roots, found me. She seemed... startled. Flustered, even. She quickly ushered me out of the room, insisting it was a restricted area."

Ethyl's gaze returned to us, her eyes filled with a mix of fear and determination. "I've been wary ever since," she admitted, her voice barely above a whisper. "Something about that room... it didn't sit right with me. And Dori's reaction only confirmed my suspicions."

Her revelation was interesting, to say the least. A potion-making operation hidden within a charity organization? It was a lead, and one we couldn't afford to ignore. We thanked Ethyl for her information, promising to look into At the Roots and the mysterious Dori Messel.

Chapter Twelve

As the evening settled in, painting the sky with hues of deep purples and blues, Thorn, Meri, and I reconvened in the comfort of our home. The events of the day hung in the air around us, a palpable weight that seemed to seep into the very walls of the house. We gathered in the living room, the soft glow of the lamps casting long shadows across the room, creating an atmosphere that mirrored our somber moods.

Thorn, ever the lawman, was visibly troubled by the idea of investigating At the Roots without the proper legal permissions. He sat in his favorite armchair, his strong arms crossed over his chest, his brow furrowed in a deep frown. His gaze was distant, lost in thought as he contemplated our next move.

"We can't just barge into their premises," he finally said, his voice carrying a note of stern caution. "We need more than just suspicions and hearsay. We need solid, undeniable evidence."

His words echoed in the quiet room, a stark reminder of the delicate balance we were trying to maintain. We were walking a fine line, and one misstep could jeopardize everything.

I understood his reservations, but the urgency of the situation was too great to ignore. "We won't storm in," I reassured him, meeting his gaze steadily. "Meri and I will go, quietly, after hours. We'll be as discreet as possible."

Thorn didn't look entirely convinced, but he didn't voice any further objections. He gave us a stern reminder to be careful before we set off.

The drive to At the Roots was a silent affair, the only sound being the gentle purr of the car's engine as we navigated Coventry's streets. The city had settled into its nighttime rhythm, the usual bustle replaced by a serene quietude that seemed to blanket everything in its peaceful embrace. The buildings and houses we passed were mere silhouettes against the night sky, their details obscured by the cloak of darkness.

We parked the car a few blocks away from our destination, opting to approach the rest of the way on foot to avoid drawing attention. The cool night air was a sharp contrast to the car's warm interior, sending a shiver down my spine as we stepped out into the darkness.

We moved stealthily, sticking to the shadows as we made our way towards the building. The streets were deserted, the only sounds being our soft footfalls and the distant hoot of an owl. The building loomed ahead of us, its darkened windows and silent facade giving nothing away. We paused at the edge of the property, taking a moment to survey our surroundings before proceeding.

Breaking into At the Roots was a task that required both subtlety and a touch of magic. The building was securely locked, but with a whispered incantation and a flick of my wrist, the front door's lock yielded with a soft click. We slipped inside, the door closing behind us with a near-silent thud.

The interior of the building was shrouded in darkness, the only illumination coming from the faint glow of the streetlights outside. We moved cautiously, our footsteps muffled by the thick carpet as we navigated the dimly lit space. The building was eerily silent, the only sounds being our soft breathing and the distant hum of the city outside.

We made our way towards the back of the building, guided by the faint scent of herbs and the unmistakable hum of magic. As we approached a particular door, the scent of herbs grew stronger, and the hum of magic more intense. This was it.

The door was locked, but I was prepared. With another whispered incantation and a flick of my wrist, the lock gave way. We pushed the door open to reveal a room that had been transformed into a makeshift laboratory.

Tables were cluttered with vials, herbs, and various pieces of equipment. The air was thick with the scent of magic and various herbs, a potent mix that made my senses tingle. It was clear that this was where the potion-making operation took place. The room was a hive of illicit activity, the evidence of potion-making undeniable in the array of ingredients and equipment scattered around.

With the evidence of the potion-making operation right in front of us, I quickly pulled out my phone and began to take photos. The flash from the camera briefly illuminated the room, casting stark shadows against the walls. Each image captured the illicit operation in stark detail, from the cluttered tables filled with vials and herbs to the complex equipment scattered around the room.

Once I had documented the room thoroughly, Meri and I continued our search. We moved through the building quietly, our senses on high alert for any signs of further illicit activity. Our search led us to an office, a room that was starkly different from the makeshift lab we had just left.

The office was neat and organized, with a large desk dominating the room. On the desk, we found a ledger. It was a thick book, filled with pages of detailed records. As I flipped through the pages, I quickly realized that it was a record of transactions - illegal potion ingredients being bought and sold.

One entry, in particular, caught my eye. It was a record of a recent purchase of the same rare herb that had been used in the attack on Isadora. The implications were chilling. Not only was At the Roots involved in the illegal potion trade, but they were also linked to the attack on Isadora.

As I continued to flip through the ledger, the details of the potion-making operation became increasingly clear. The ledger was meticulously maintained, with entries detailing the names of the buyers, the quantities of ingredients purchased, and the dates of the transactions. It was a damning record of the illicit activities taking place under the guise of a charity.

One set of initials, in particular, caught my eye. "MT" appeared multiple times throughout the ledger. The initials were familiar, and it took me a moment to place them. They matched those of the mayor of Coventry.

I felt a chill run down my spine as the realization hit me. Could the mayor be involved in this? The implications were staggering. I quickly snapped photos of the pages where "MT" was mentioned, ensuring that we had evidence of the connection.

I quickly took photos of the ledger, ensuring that each page was captured clearly. With the evidence secured, we carefully replaced the ledger and turned to leave.

Just as I was about to walk out of the office, Meri hopped up onto the desk, his attention focused on a piece of paper. I watched as he pawed at it, nudging it towards me. Curious, I picked it up and quickly scanned the contents. It was a letter from the mayor to the charity organization, requesting a substantial donation to his campaign fund.

My eyebrows shot up in surprise. This was a significant find. I quickly pulled out my phone and snapped a few pictures of the letter, making sure to capture every detail. Once I was sure I had a clear record, I carefully replaced the letter exactly where Meri had found it.

"Good find, Meri," I murmured, giving him a quick scratch behind the ears. He purred in response, his tail flicking in satisfaction. With our evidence collected, we finally made our exit, leaving the office and the secrets it held behind.

Before we could make our exit from the building, Meri turned to me, his eyes gleaming in the dim light. "You should run for mayor," he said, his voice serious. I stopped in my tracks, turning to look at him in surprise.

"What?" I asked, taken aback by the sudden suggestion. "Meri, I can't even lead the coven anymore. Who would vote for me?"

Meri huffed, his tail flicking in annoyance. "You lack ambition," he accused, his gaze unwavering.

I crossed my arms over my chest, meeting his gaze head-on. "I've started two successful businesses, Meri. I think that shows plenty of ambition."

Meri snorted, clearly unimpressed. "Selling donuts next to a coffee shop isn't, like, hard," he retorted, his tone dismissive.

I opened my mouth to argue further, but then thought better of it. We were still in the midst of an illicit potion-making operation, after all. "We are not having this discussion here, Meri," I said firmly, turning to leave.

Meri huffed again but followed me out, the debate temporarily shelved. Meri was nothing if not persistent, and I had a feeling this wouldn't be the last I heard of his mayoral ambitions for me.

Just as we were about to slip back into the cover of darkness, a sudden burst of light flooded the area. Security lights, previously dormant, now illuminated the entire property like a stage under a spotlight. I froze, my heart pounding in my chest. I had been so engrossed in Meri's chatter about my potential mayoral campaign that I hadn't noticed our obfuscation spell was fading.

To make matters worse, the distant hum of a car engine grew louder, and I turned to see the familiar sight of a deputy's cruiser turning onto the street. Panic surged through me, but I forced myself to think. With my magic already stretched thin, I had two options: cast a new obfuscation spell or erase our presence from the security camera footage.

I glanced up, spotting the cameras that were undoubtedly recording our every move. Making a split-second decision, I chose to erase us from the footage. I quickly muttered the incantation, pouring the last of my energy into the spell.

With the spell cast, there was no time left for hesitation. I grabbed Meri, tucking him under my arm, and we took off running. The sudden burst of movement startled him, and he let out a disgruntled squawk, his claws digging into my arm through my shirt.

"Quiet, Meri!" I hissed, darting around the corner of a building. The security lights cast long, distorted shadows that seemed to chase us, adding to the urgency of our escape. The sound of the deputy's cruiser was growing louder, the hum of the engine echoing ominously in the still night air.

Meri, despite his initial surprise, quickly caught on to the situation. He stopped squawking, but I could hear him muttering under his breath, a string of complaints that would have been amusing under different circumstances. "This is undignified... I'm not built for running... I should have stayed in the car..."

I ignored his complaints, focusing on staying out of sight. We darted through alleyways, slipped behind buildings, and even ducked into a dense thicket of bushes at one point. My heart pounded in my chest, adrenaline fueling my movements. Every sound seemed amplified, every shadow a potential threat.

Finally, after what felt like an eternity, the sound of the cruiser faded. We had managed to evade the deputy. Panting heavily, I slowed to a walk, allowing Meri to hop down from my arms. He shook himself off, shooting me a disgruntled look, but I could only offer him a weak smile in return. That had been far too close for comfort.

"I could have run myself, you know," Meri said as we approached my car.

I fumbled with the keys, my hands shaking from the adrenaline. "Weren't you just saying you aren't built for running?"

"Excited utterances. Not admissible in court."

"They absolutely are."

He harrumphed. "What I mean is that of course I am built for running. I'm a cat. I am a hunting and running machine, Kinsley. An apex predator."

"That said he wished he'd stayed in the car."

"You were squeezing me."

"It was a reflex. I was worried we'd get caught, so I scooped you up and ran. I realize now that you probably could have run faster if I'd just let you... but I was trying to protect you."

"Don't make it weird," Meri said as he settled into the passenger seat.

"I think we're already there, friend."

"Whatever."

"Indeed," I said with a laugh and drove us home.

Chapter Thirteen

The sight of Thorn waiting anxiously by the front door as Meri and I pulled into the driveway was both a relief and a cause for concern. His arms were crossed over his chest, his brow furrowed in worry. As soon as we stepped out of the car, he was by our side, his relief palpable.

"I was about to call the station," he admitted, his voice tight. "Someone reported a break-in at At the Roots. I didn't want to risk calling you in case you were hiding, but I've been worried sick."

I felt a pang of guilt at his words. I hadn't meant to worry him, but I knew he was right. Our actions had been reckless, and we had been incredibly lucky to escape without being caught.

"I'm sorry, Thorn," I said, meeting his gaze. "But we found something."

His annoyance was quickly replaced by curiosity as I showed him the photos and explained what we had discovered. Despite his initial frustration, he couldn't deny the significance of our findings. However, he was quick to remind me of the risks we had taken.

"This is big, Kinsley," he said, his voice serious. "But you can't just break into places like that. It's illegal, and it's dangerous. And even with this evidence, we still don't have enough for a search warrant. What you saw was obtained illegally."

I knew he was right, but it was still frustrating. We were so close to uncovering the truth, yet it felt like we were still miles away. But Thorn was right. We needed to proceed carefully, and that meant talking to the mayor. Despite the late hour, we agreed to confront him first thing in the morning.

***

As we stepped into the mayor's office, the secretary's gaze fell upon us, her eyes narrowing in a clear show of disapproval. She was a stern-looking woman, her lips pressed into a thin line that suggested she was not in the habit of smiling often. Her gaze swept over us, taking in our appearance with a critical eye before she finally spoke.

"Can I help you?" she asked, her tone as frosty as her demeanor.

"We're here to see Mayor Taylor," Thorn replied, his voice steady and calm.

The secretary's eyebrows shot up in surprise. "Do you have an appointment?" she asked, her tone suggesting she already knew the answer.

"No, but this is important," Thorn insisted, his tone firm.

The secretary looked unimpressed. "The mayor is a busy man," she said, her tone dismissive. "He doesn't have time for unscheduled meetings."

Thorn didn't back down. "This is a matter of urgent town business," he said, meeting her gaze head-on. "I'm sure the mayor wouldn't want to delay dealing with it."

There was a tense moment of silence as the secretary and Thorn locked gazes. Then, with a sigh of resignation, she picked up the phone and dialed a number. After a brief conversation, she hung up and gestured towards a set of large wooden doors.

"The mayor will see you now," she said, her tone begrudging.

With a nod of thanks, Thorn and I made our way towards the mayor's office.

The imposing figure of Mayor Miles Taylor greeted us as we entered his office. He was a man who wore his authority like a tailored suit, every word and gesture radiating an air of command. His desk was a fortress of paperwork, a testament to the responsibilities he held. Yet, as we began to lay out our evidence, I could see the first cracks appearing in his confident facade.

"Mayor Taylor," Thorn began, his voice steady and firm. "We've been conducting an investigation into a recent attack on a local witch. Our findings have led us here."

The mayor's eyes widened slightly, a flicker of surprise crossing his features before he quickly masked it. "That's a serious accusation, Sheriff," he replied, his voice steady but a hint of unease creeping into his tone. "I hope you have evidence to back it up."

Thorn nodded, and I began to lay out the photographs and documents we had gathered. As I spread them out on his desk, I watched the mayor's face closely. His eyes darted nervously from one piece of evidence to the next, and I could see beads of sweat beginning to form on his forehead.

"I... I don't understand," he stammered, his gaze locked onto the photographs. "I have nothing to do with this. This is all a misunderstanding."

Despite his words, his nervousness was palpable. We had struck a nerve, and we both knew it. "Thank you for your time," Thorn said. "We'll be in touch."

As we left his office, Thorn turned to me. "We're on the right track," he said, a determined look in his eyes. "Let's get back to the station and keep digging. And let's have Jeremy keep a subtle eye on the mayor's movements. Something tells me he's not as innocent as he claims."

Returning to the sheriff's station, we found Jeremy at his desk, engrossed in a stack of paperwork. He looked up as we approached, his eyebrows raising in question.

"Jeremy," Thorn began, leaning against the edge of the desk. "We need your help with something."

Jeremy set his pen down, giving us his full attention. "Sure, what's up?"

"We just had a meeting with Mayor Taylor," I chimed in, crossing my arms over my chest. "We confronted him with the evidence we've gathered so far. He denied everything, of course, but he was clearly nervous."

Jeremy's eyebrows shot up in surprise. "The mayor? You think he's involved?"

"We're not sure yet," Thorn replied, his expression serious. "But we need to keep an eye on him. We need you to do it subtly, though. We can't afford to spook him."

Jeremy nodded, understanding the gravity of the situation. "Understood. I'll keep a low profile. Anything specific I should be looking for?"

"Any unusual behavior, meetings, or contacts," I answered. "And keep an eye out for any connection to At the Roots charity or any illicit potion activity."

"Got it," Jeremy said, already reaching for his notepad to jot down the details. "I'll start right away."

Thorn and I found ourselves back at the sheriff's station, hunched over a desk cluttered with a variety of documents and a laptop that was humming with activity. Our focus was on Mayor Taylor, a man who had always presented himself as a humble public servant. But as we delved deeper into his background and recent activities, a different picture began to form.

We started with the most accessible information - public records. Property records, for instance, were public and showed that Mayor Taylor owned a sprawling estate in one of Coventry's most exclusive neighborhoods. The value of the property alone was several times his annual salary as mayor, and that didn't even take into account the cost of upkeep, staff, and utilities.

Then there was his car - a high-end model that was more at home in the pages of a luxury magazine than the parking lot of Coventry's town hall. The car was registered in his name, and a quick online search gave us an idea of its hefty price tag.

As for his financial records, we didn't have direct access to his bank accounts or credit card statements. However, Thorn had contacts at the bank who were able to provide some insight. They couldn't give us specific numbers, but they confirmed that Mayor Taylor frequently made large transactions that seemed inconsistent with his official income.

We then shifted our focus to Mayor Taylor's online presence. In this digital age, social media had become a powerful tool for politicians to engage with their constituents, and Mayor Taylor was no exception. His accounts were a blend of professional and personal, a curated showcase of his life as a public servant and as an individual.

His professional posts were what one would expect from a politician - updates on local policies, photos from community events, and messages of encouragement or solidarity during challenging times. But it was his personal posts that caught our attention.

Mayor Taylor seemed to have a penchant for travel. Almost every weekend, his social media accounts would be updated with photos and anecdotes from various destinations. Sometimes it was a scenic coastal town, other times a bustling city or a tranquil countryside. The locations varied, but the frequency of these trips was striking.

These weren't just day trips either. From the timestamps on his posts and the variety of locations, it was clear that Mayor Taylor was spending entire weekends away from Coventry. This was unusual for a public servant whose role typically required a strong local presence and availability.

Moreover, these trips didn't come cheap. The destinations he chose were known for their high living costs, and the activities he engaged in - fine dining, luxury accommodations, and various leisure activities - all pointed towards a significant expenditure.

Thorn and I shared a look, our thoughts aligning as we reviewed the information we'd gathered. It was intriguing, certainly, and it painted a picture of Mayor Taylor that was far from flattering. But it was all circumstantial, nothing concrete enough to act upon.

"We need more," Thorn said, his voice firm. "Something solid, something that directly links Taylor to these activities."

I nodded in agreement, my mind already racing with potential avenues of investigation. "We should talk to the people at At the Roots," I suggested. "The employees, the volunteers. Someone there might know something."

Thorn's brow furrowed in thought. "That's a good idea," he said. "But we'll have to be careful. If Dori Messel is there, she'll likely try to interfere."

I picked up my phone, already dialing the number for At the Roots. "Then let's make sure she's not there," I said, holding the phone to my ear. "I'll call and ask to speak to her. If she's out, we go in."

A woman answered, her voice polite and professional. I asked to speak with Dori Messel, keeping my tone casual. The woman on the other end of the line informed me that Dori was out of the office for the morning. This was the opportunity we wanted.

I thanked the woman and hung up, turning to Thorn with a determined look. "Dori's out for the morning," I relayed, already moving towards the door. "We should head over to At the Roots now."

"Let's go," he agreed, his tone matching my own sense of urgency. We had a narrow window of opportunity, and we intended to make the most of it.

As Thorn and I entered the bustling office of At the Roots, we were greeted by a bright-eyed receptionist. Her face lit up with excitement when I introduced myself, and the mention of my family name seemed to add an extra spark to her enthusiasm.

"Oh, it's wonderful that you're interested in our cause!" she exclaimed, clasping her hands together.

"We could always use more help. Come, let me show you around."

She led us through the office, her steps brisk and eager. The office was a hive of activity, with employees and volunteers busily working at their desks. As we moved through the room, I noticed Meri had slipped in, his dark form darting between desks and chairs.

Amidst the hum of activity, we approached a young woman who was meticulously sorting through a towering stack of papers.

"Excuse me," Thorn began, his voice friendly and disarming. "We're interested in learning more about the work you do here. We're considering getting involved."

The woman looked up, surprise flickering across her features. She glanced around the room, her gaze darting to her colleagues before she leaned in closer. "Well," she started, her voice dropping to a hushed whisper, "we're not really supposed to talk about it. It's all very hush-hush, you know? But they pay us really well, so no one really questions it."

Next, we turned our attention to a man seated at a computer. His fingers flew across the keyboard, his focus entirely on his screen until Thorn cleared his throat. He looked up, offering a polite smile as he asked, "Can I help you?"

"We're just interested in the work you do here," I chimed in, my tone matching Thorn's casual friendliness. "It seems like a great cause."

The man's smile faltered slightly, his gaze flicking to his screen before meeting mine. "Yeah, it's... it's good work," he admitted, his voice tinged with hesitation. "But we're supposed to keep it on the down-low. The pay, though... it's more than generous."

As we moved from one employee to the next, the narrative remained the same. Each person we spoke to confirmed the secrecy surrounding their work and the unusually high compensation they received in exchange for their silence.

Thorn and I stepped away from the bustling office space, finding a quiet corner where we could discuss our findings. The openness of the employees was puzzling, their willingness to divulge sensitive information about their work was unexpected, to say the least.

"Something doesn't add up," Thorn murmured, his brow furrowed in thought. "Why would they be so forthcoming about their secret work and the large payments?"

Before I could respond, a familiar voice piped up from below. "You're welcome," Meri said, a smug tone in his voice as he sauntered over to join us. His eyes sparkled with mischief, and a knowing grin spread across his face.

I blinked in surprise, turning to look down at my familiar. "Meri, did you...?"

His grin widened, and he gave a nonchalant shrug. "Well, someone had to get them to talk."

I couldn't help but laugh, shaking my head in disbelief. "You sneaky little... Well, thank you, Meri."

With Meri's powers at play, the pieces of the puzzle finally fell into place. The employees weren't just being unusually candid - they were under the influence of Meri's charm. It was a risky move, but it had paid off.

As Thorn and I retreated further into the quiet corner, we began to piece together the larger picture. The revelations from the employees and volunteers painted a troubling image of the operations at At the Roots. The charity was paying its staff substantial sums of money to maintain their silence, a fact that raised more questions than it answered.

"Where would a charity get the funds to pay off their employees like this?" I mused aloud, my brows furrowed in thought. "It doesn't make sense."

Thorn nodded, his expression serious. "Unless," he began, his voice low, "the charity isn't the main operation. What if it's just a front for something bigger?"

It was disconcerting. The idea that Mayor Taylor could be involved in a larger criminal organization was a daunting prospect. But it made sense. The large payments, the secrecy, the illicit potion-making operation - all these elements pointed to a criminal enterprise far more extensive than we had initially suspected.

"We need to tread carefully," Thorn warned, his gaze meeting mine. "If we're right about this, we're dealing with something much bigger than we initially thought."

Chapter Fourteen

The shrill ring of my phone cut through our conversation, startling us both. I quickly fished it out of my pocket, glancing at the caller ID. It was the hospital. My heart leapt into my throat as I answered, my voice barely above a whisper.

"Hello?"

The news on the other end of the line was like a ray of sunshine breaking through the storm clouds. Isadora had finally woken up from her coma. A wave of relief washed over me, so intense that I had to lean against the wall for support.

"Thorn," I managed to say, my voice choked with emotion. "Isadora's awake."

Without wasting another moment, we left At the Roots, rushing to the hospital. The drive was a blur, my mind filled with a whirlwind of thoughts and emotions.

Upon entering the hospital room, the sight of Isadora, awake and alert, was a relief. Her face was pale against the stark white of the hospital sheets, but her eyes were open and focused. I moved to her bedside, reaching out to gently take her hand.

"Isadora," I began, my voice soft, but steady. "I'm so glad to see you awake. How are you feeling?"

She offered a weak smile, her fingers squeezing mine in a feeble grip. "I've been better," she admitted, her voice barely above a whisper. "But I'll manage. How's my daughter?"

"She's doing well," I assured her, offering a comforting smile. "She's been strong, just like her mother."

A flicker of relief passed over Isadora's face, but it was quickly replaced by a look of fatigue. It was then that Thorn stepped forward, his expression serious.

"Isadora," he began, his tone gentle but firm. "I hate to have to do this so soon after you've woken up, but we need to ask you some questions. The investigation into your attack... it's urgent."

Isadora's gaze shifted to Thorn, her eyes reflecting understanding. "I know," she said, her voice steady despite her condition. "I'll do my best to help."

As Isadora began to recount her memories, her voice was soft, her words slow and measured. It was clear that the events leading up to the attack were a jumbled mess in her mind, the details fragmented and hazy. Yet, she pressed on, determined to provide us with as much information as she could.

"I had been investigating... my family's heirloom," she began, her brow furrowing in concentration. "It had been stolen... and I was trying to find it."

Her voice trailed off, her gaze distant as she delved into her fragmented memories. After a moment, she continued, her voice growing stronger.

"But it wasn't just the heirloom," she said, her gaze meeting ours. "There were other thefts too. Rare and valuable magical artifacts... from museums, private collections... all over the country."

Her words hung in the air, painting a picture of a series of crimes far larger than we had initially suspected. But before we could delve deeper, Isadora raised a hand, her expression serious.

"But you need to understand," she said, her gaze steady. "My memory... it's not what it used to be. Everything's a bit fuzzy, a bit... out of reach. I can't guarantee that everything I'm telling you is accurate."

Despite the lack of concrete information, her account provided us with a new lead to follow. We thanked Isadora for her help, promising to do everything within our power to bring her attacker to justice.

Our conversation with Isadora was interrupted by the arrival of a stern-looking nurse. She entered the room with a brisk efficiency, her gaze sweeping over us with a clear message - visiting hours were over.

"Time for your medicine, Isadora," she announced, moving to the bedside with a small tray in her hands. She then turned her gaze to us, her expression softening slightly. "You should let her rest now. She needs her strength."

I nodded, understanding the importance of Isadora's recovery. I leaned in, giving Isadora's hand a gentle squeeze. "Call me if you need anything, okay?" I told her, my voice soft.

Isadora gave a weak nod, her eyes already beginning to droop with exhaustion. With a final wave, Thorn and I left the room, leaving Isadora in the capable hands of her nurse.

Once outside the hospital, Thorn turned to me. "I could use some food," he said, his stomach growling. I chuckled, nodding in agreement. The day had been long and eventful already, and we both needed a moment to regroup and process everything we had learned. So, we decided to head back to town and get something to eat.

***

We found ourselves at a pop-up restaurant, a food truck parked in the bustling square, serving up delicious Korean tacos. The aroma of the food was mouthwatering, and we quickly placed our orders, finding a nearby bench to sit and eat.

As we dug into our meals, our conversation naturally drifted back to the case. Between bites of spicy bulgogi and tangy kimchi, we began to piece together a theory. The mayor's suspicious activities, the secretive operations at At the Roots, the thefts of magical artifacts that Isadora had mentioned - they all seemed to point towards a larger criminal organization.

"Think about it," Thorn said, gesturing with a half-eaten taco. "The mayor's living beyond his means, there's shady stuff going on at the charity, and now these thefts... It's all too much to be a coincidence."

I nodded, my mind whirling with the implications. "And if the mayor is involved with this organization, it could explain how they're funding their operations."

Our conversation was interrupted by the sound of Thorn's phone ringing. He answered it, listened for a moment, then hung up with a sigh. "That was Jeremy. He's been keeping an eye on the mayor, like we asked. Says he's been acting nervous, making a lot of phone calls."

We finished our meal in thoughtful silence, each of us lost in our own thoughts. As we got up to leave, Thorn turned to me. "We should talk to the curator at the local museum," he suggested. "If these thefts are as widespread as Isadora suggested, they might have some information that could help us."

I agreed, and we decided to make that our next stop in our investigation. The day was far from over, and we had a lot more ground to cover.

The museum of Coventry was a place I had rarely visited, despite its close proximity to my home. It was a treasure trove of the town's history, a history that was intertwined with my own lineage, yet I had seldom taken the time to delve into it. Today, however, as Thorn and I meandered through the labyrinth of exhibits, waiting for the curator to finish his phone call, I found myself unexpectedly drawn to a particular display.

It was an exhibit dedicated to my own residence, the infamous Hangman's House, and its deep-rooted connection to the Coventry Witch Trials. I was taken aback, my heart skipping a beat as I saw photographs of my ancestral home on display, accompanied by detailed information about my families - the Tuttlesmith witches on my mother's side and the Skeenbauer witches on my father's. The exhibit even showcased photographs of the family crypt nestled in the heart of Coventry Cemetery, a place that held a chilling history of its own.

As I stood there, rooted to the spot, I found myself enveloped in a strange sensation. Seeing my personal history, my lineage, laid out for public consumption was an unsettling experience. It was as if a part of my identity, a part that was deeply personal and private, was suddenly exposed for all to see. A shiver ran down my spine, the images of the crypt stirring up memories of the horrors it contained.

As Thorn and I stood there, lost in the eerie familiarity of the exhibit, our quiet contemplation was broken by the arrival of the museum curator. He was a tall man, his stature accentuated by a lean frame. His hair, peppered with gray, was neatly combed back, and a pair of spectacles perched on the bridge of his nose, lending him a scholarly air. His demeanor was calm, exuding an aura of quiet authority that seemed to fit seamlessly with the hallowed halls of the museum.

"Good afternoon," he greeted us, his voice warm and welcoming. His eyes, a soft shade of brown, held a spark of curiosity as he extended a hand towards us. "I'm Dr. Harold Finch, the curator of the museum. I understand you had some questions?"

Thorn stepped forward, shaking Dr. Finch's hand firmly. "Yes, thank you for meeting with us, Dr. Finch," he began, his tone professional. "I'm Sheriff Thorn Wilson, and this is Kinsley Wilson. We're currently investigating a series of thefts involving rare and valuable magical artifacts."

Dr. Finch's eyebrows rose slightly at this, but he gestured for us to follow him into his office. As we settled into the chairs opposite his desk, Thorn continued, "We have reason to believe that one of the stolen artifacts may have ended up in a local pawn shop. We were hoping you could help us confirm this."

Dr. Finch leaned back in his chair, his fingers steepled in front of him as he absorbed the information we presented. His gaze was thoughtful, his eyes flicking between Thorn and me as we laid out the details of our investigation.

After a moment, he leaned forward, his interest piqued by one of the photos we had brought up. It was a clear, detailed image of the artifact we had found in Fred's pawn shop. His eyes narrowed slightly as he studied the photo, his fingers tapping thoughtfully on the surface of his desk.

"Yes," he finally confirmed, his voice steady and certain. "This artifact matches the description of one that was stolen from our collection. It's a unique piece, part of a private collection that was donated to us a few years ago."

"Thank you, Dr. Finch," Thorn said, his tone appreciative. "Your assistance has been invaluable. We'll do everything we can to recover the stolen artifacts and bring those responsible to justice."

As we left the museum, Thorn's phone buzzed, interrupting the quiet of the afternoon. He glanced at the screen before answering. "Jeremy," he greeted, his tone professional.

I watched Thorn's face as he listened to the information being relayed on the other end of the line. His eyebrows knitted together in a thoughtful frown. "Multiple donations to At the Roots from Richard Blackwell?" he echoed, his gaze flicking to me.

At the mention of the name, recognition sparked in my mind. Richard Blackwell. The wealthy businessman who had once promised to help Isadora fund the children's wing at the library, only to back out at the last minute. A man of means, with a reputation for being less than reliable.

Thorn ended the call and turned to me, his expression serious. "Jeremy's been doing some digging while keeping an eye on Mayor Taylor. He's found a connection between Richard Blackwell and At the Roots."

Chapter Fifteen

Thorn and I sat in the living room, our eyes scanning the social media posts on our respective devices. A charity event at Blackwell's mansion was the talk of the town, and the buzz was impossible to ignore.

"Look at this," I said, turning my phone towards Thorn. The screen displayed a post from Blackwell himself, hinting at the showcase of his rare artifacts. "He's going to display some of his collection at the event."

Thorn leaned in, studying the post. "That's unusual," he mused, his brow furrowing in thought. "Why would he suddenly decide to showcase his collection?"

"Maybe he's trying to impress the donors," I suggested. "Or maybe there's something else going on."

Thorn nodded, his gaze thoughtful. "Either way, this could be a good opportunity for us. We could attend the event, pose as potential donors. It would give us a chance to observe Blackwell and maybe even get a look at these artifacts."

I agreed, feeling a spark of excitement. This was a lead, a chance to gather more information. "All right,"

I said, standing up. "Let's do it. We'll need to dress the part, though. This isn't exactly a casual event."

Thorn chuckled, rising to his feet. "I think we can manage that," he said, a glint of amusement in his eyes. "Let's see what we can do to blend in with Coventry's elite."

The prospect of viewing these artifacts firsthand was an opportunity we couldn't pass up. We chose our outfits carefully, aiming for a balance of elegance and understated sophistication. We were about to step into the lion's den, and there was no telling what we would find.

***

Thorn and I arrived at Blackwell's mansion, a grand edifice that stood as a testament to his wealth and power. The mansion was a hive of activity, the air filled with the hum of conversation and the soft strains of a string quartet playing in the background. The scent of expensive perfume and gourmet food wafted through the air, mingling with the crisp aroma of champagne.

We stepped into the grand ballroom, our eyes taking in the opulent surroundings. Crystal chandeliers hung from the high ceiling, casting a warm, golden glow over the room. The walls were adorned with exquisite pieces of art, and the floor was a polished marble that reflected the light in a dazzling display.

The room was filled with Coventry's elite, their expensive attire and polished manners a stark contrast to the more down-to-earth residents we were accustomed to dealing with. We exchanged pleasantries with a few of the guests, our eyes constantly scanning the room for any signs of Blackwell's collection.

As we moved through the crowd, we subtly observed the guests. We were looking for any signs of unusual behavior, any clue that could point us towards the artifacts Blackwell had hinted at in his posts. We knew we had to tread carefully, to avoid drawing attention to ourselves.

After navigating through the throng of guests, Thorn and I finally found ourselves standing before a carefully curated display of artifacts. Each item was encased in a glass box, meticulously arranged on a long table draped in a rich, velvet cloth. The artifacts ranged from ancient scrolls to ornate jewelry, each piece a testament to Blackwell's discerning taste and his penchant for the exotic and rare.

Thorn and I took our time, our eyes carefully scanning each artifact. We were looking for anything that might hint at a connection to our investigation, any sign that these items were more than just a wealthy man's collection. We studied the intricate designs of an ancient amulet, the faded script on a centuries-old scroll, the delicate craftsmanship of a jeweled dagger.

However, as we moved from one artifact to the next, it became increasingly clear that all the items on display were legal. Each piece was accompanied by a small plaque detailing its provenance, a clear indication that Blackwell had taken the necessary steps to ensure the legality of his displayed collection. It was a disappointing realization, but not entirely unexpected. Blackwell was a shrewd man, and it was unlikely he would risk displaying illegal artifacts in such a public setting.

Despite this, our visit was far from fruitless. Being in Blackwell's mansion, seeing his collection firsthand and observing his interactions with the other guests painted a clearer picture of the man we were dealing with. It was a valuable insight that would undoubtedly aid us in our ongoing investigation.

Despite the initial setback, I wasn't ready to concede defeat just yet. As the event carried on, the hum of conversation and clinking of glasses providing a steady background noise, I decided to take matters into my own hands. Using my magic in a subtle and unobtrusive manner, I cast a spell of detection. This spell, a delicate pulse of magical energy, would allow me to sense any hidden or concealed rooms within the mansion's grand structure.

The spell guided me towards a seemingly ordinary door, inconspicuously tucked away in a quiet corner of the mansion. Ensuring that no prying eyes were watching, I gently nudged the door open and slipped inside, the door closing quietly behind me.

The room I found myself in was a stark contrast to the opulence of the rest of the mansion. It was smaller, more intimate, and filled with shelves upon shelves of artifacts that were even more impressive than those on public display. Ancient tomes with worn leather bindings, ornate jewelry embedded with precious stones, and a myriad of other items filled the room, each one radiating a powerful aura of magic that was almost palpable.

As I moved through the room, my eyes were drawn to a particular item - a vial containing a potion that was all too familiar. The sight of it sent a jolt of realization through me. This was the rare potion we had been investigating, the same potion that had been used in the attack on Isadora. The presence of it here, in Blackwell's private collection, confirmed our suspicions. Blackwell was not merely a collector of rare artifacts; he was involved in something far more sinister and dangerous.

I took out my phone to record whatever evidence I could. Once that was done, we left before anyone could find us and ask us what we were doing.

As we stepped out of the Blackwell mansion, the night air was a stark contrast to the air-conditioned opulence we had just left behind. The evening was hot and sticky, the kind of summer night where the heat seemed to cling to your skin. We walked in silence towards our car, parked discreetly a short distance away.

Once we were safely ensconced in the vehicle, away from prying eyes and ears, I turned to Thorn. "Blackwell is involved in this," I stated, my voice firm. The evidence was too compelling to ignore. "The potion in his private collection, his ties to At the Roots... it's too much of a coincidence."

Thorn nodded, his gaze focused on the mansion receding in the rearview mirror. "I agree," he said, his voice equally firm. "But we need more than coincidences. We need concrete evidence if we're going to expose him."

The drive home was filled with a tense silence as we both contemplated the implications of our findings. Whether Blackwell was part of a larger criminal organization or simply a lone wolf, it was clear that he was deeply entangled in the web of illegal activities we were investigating. The challenge now was to gather enough evidence to prove it, to expose the truth hidden beneath the veneer of charity and philanthropy.

Chapter Sixteen

As the morning sun bathed the kitchen in a warm, golden light, Thorn and I found ourselves engrossed in a deep discussion over breakfast. The aroma of freshly brewed coffee mingled with the scent of sizzling bacon and eggs, creating a comforting backdrop to our conversation. Meri, ever the opportunist, was perched on a nearby chair, his bright eyes fixed on the plate of bacon in front of me.

"Remember Blackwell's promise to fund the new children's library?" Thorn asked, his gaze thoughtful as he stirred his coffee. "And how he suddenly backed out?"

I nodded, the memory fresh in my mind. It had been a significant blow to Isadora, who had been deeply invested in the project. "Yes, I remember," I replied, my mind already racing with the potential implications. "You think there's a connection?"

Thorn shrugged, his expression contemplative. "It's worth exploring," he said. "We should talk to Isadora. She might have some insights."

I agreed, and we decided to visit Isadora later that morning. Breaking off a piece of bacon, I tossed it to Meri who caught it mid-air, his tail swishing in delight.

***

The sterile, antiseptic-scented hallways of the hospital were a stark contrast to the cozy familiarity of our home. As Thorn and I navigated the hallways, the smell of disinfectant was a constant reminder of the battles fought and won within these walls. We finally arrived at Isadora's room, finding her in a state of noticeable improvement compared to the previous day. However, she was still a far cry from her usual vibrant self.

Upon our arrival, Isadora's mother and daughter were already at her bedside, their faces brightening at the sight of us. Isadora, however, looked at them with a gentle firmness in her eyes.

"Mom, Isabella," she began, her voice soft but steady. "Why don't you two go grab something to eat from the cafeteria? I'll be fine here with Thorn and Kinsley."

Her mother looked as if she was about to protest, but a reassuring nod from Isadora silenced any objections. Isabella, her young face filled with concern, gave her mother a quick hug before following her grandmother out of the room. As the door closed behind them, Isadora turned her attention back to us, ready to find out why we were there.

"We didn't mean to interrupt," Thorn began, his tone gentle. "But we have some questions about the library project. Specifically, about the funding."

Isadora's forehead wrinkled in concentration; her gaze distant as she tried to dredge up the memories from her still hazy mind. "The library project..." she murmured, her voice trailing off. "There were... difficulties with the funding, yes."

Thorn nodded, leaning forward slightly. "We were wondering if you could tell us anything about Richard Blackwell's involvement in the project."

At the mention of Richard's name, Isadora's reaction was immediate. Her eyes widened, and a look of fear crossed her face. She recoiled slightly, her hands clutching at the hospital sheets. "Richard..." she whispered, her voice trembling. "I... I don't know why, but his name... it scares me." Her reaction was a clear indication that there was something about Richard that deeply unsettled her.

Thorn cleared his throat. "Isadora," he began, his voice carrying a note of seriousness, "we have reason to believe that Blackwell might have used his promised donation as leverage. We think he might have been trying to pressure you to back off from your investigation into the stolen artifacts."

I nodded in agreement, my gaze fixed on Isadora. "Does that sound plausible to you, Isadora? Could Blackwell have had a reason to want you to stop your investigation?"

Isadora's eyes widened slightly at our words, and she took a moment to process the information. Her gaze flickered between Thorn and me.

Isadora's gaze seemed to drift away from us, her eyes taking on a far-off look as if she was delving deep into her own memories. "There was... a letter," she began, her voice barely more than a whisper. The words seemed to be pulled from her, each one a struggle as she fought against the fog of her memory. "A warning. It told me to stop my search."

Thorn and I exchanged a glance, the significance of her words not lost on us. A threatening letter could be a crucial piece of evidence, a tangible link to the person or persons behind the thefts and the attack on Isadora.

"Do you still have this letter, Isadora?" I asked, my voice gentle but insistent. I leaned forward in my chair, my gaze fixed on her.

She nodded, her eyes still distant. "Yes, I... I hid it," she admitted. "I didn't know who I could trust." She paused, her gaze flickering to a spot on the wall as if she could see the hiding place in her mind's eye. "It's in the library. There's a book... a book about infamous people. It's not a popular read. I hid the letter in there."

She paused for a moment, her brow furrowing as she tried to remember more details. "The book... it's in the history section. Third shelf from the bottom, towards the right. The title is 'Infamous Figures of the Twentieth Century.' It's a thick, hardcover book with a black and white cover."

Isadora's strength seemed to ebb away with each passing moment of our conversation. Her eyelids were heavy, her words slower, and her voice softer. It was clear that the exertion of recalling her fragmented memories was taking a toll on her. As if on cue, a nurse entered the room, her stern gaze landing on us as she announced that it was time for Isadora to rest.

"Isadora, we'll leave you to rest now," I said gently, rising from my chair. "We appreciate your help."

Thorn echoed my sentiments, adding a quiet word of thanks. Together, we exited the room, leaving Isadora in the capable hands of the hospital staff.

Our next destination was the Coventry library. Stepping into the library, we were immediately enveloped by the hushed atmosphere that was so characteristic of such places.

We made our way to the history section, following Isadora's directions to the letter. There, nestled among countless other books, we found the book titled 'Infamous Figures of the Twentieth Century.'

The letter we found within the pages of the obscure book was exactly as Isadora had described it. The words, inked in a harsh, angular script, were an unmistakable threat. The message was clear and chilling: cease her investigations or face dire consequences. The sender's address was a nondescript post office box, providing us with a tantalizing lead in our investigation.

As we stepped out of the library, we found Meri waiting for us. He was perched on a nearby bench, his eyes gleaming with an almost human-like curiosity. Thorn greeted him with a nod, a small smile tugging at the corners of his mouth. "You're right on time, Meri."

Meri tilted his head to the side, his eyes narrowing slightly in confusion. "Why's that?" he asked, his voice a low, rumbling purr.

"We're heading to the post office," Thorn explained, his tone steady and matter-of-fact. "We've come across some information that's going to require a bit of... persuasion to access. Information that, without a warrant, would require the mail clerk to break federal law. We're hoping you can help with that."

At Thorn's words, Meri's eyes lit up with excitement. A wide, mischievous grin spread across his face, revealing a row of sharp, gleaming teeth. "Sounds like fun," he said, his tail flicking back and forth in anticipation.

***

As we entered the post office, Meri hopped onto the counter with a confident leap. His eyes were locked onto the clerk behind the counter, who seemed oblivious to the magical creature in their midst. Thorn stepped forward, the threatening letter in hand. "We need some information about the person who sent this," he said, his voice steady and authoritative.

The clerk, under Meri's subtle influence, nodded and turned to their computer. Their fingers danced over the keys as they pulled up the information. After a moment, they looked up and handed Thorn a slip of paper. "The PO Box is registered to this name and address," they said.

Thorn thanked the clerk and stepped away from the counter, pulling out his phone to relay the information to dispatch. As he waited for a response, I could see the anticipation in his eyes. This could be the lead we were looking for.

I stood close enough so that I could hear what they said when they answered Thorn's inquiry. The response from dispatch was not what we had hoped for. "That name and address doesn't exist in our system," the dispatcher said, their voice crackling over the phone. "It seems to be a pseudonym or a fake."

We didn't let the setback deter us. Instead, we decided to dig deeper. We turned our attention to the postal workers, hoping that they might be able to provide us with more information about the mysterious PO Box renter.

We approached a few of the workers, explaining our situation and asking if they had noticed anything unusual. One of the workers, a middle-aged man with a friendly face, seemed to recall something.

"Yeah, there's this one person," he said, scratching his chin thoughtfully. "They've been using that PO Box quite a lot recently. Always comes in wearing a hooded sweatshirt, no matter the weather. Keeps their head down, doesn't talk much. Can't say I've ever gotten a good look at their face."

After we exited the post office, the three of us climbed back into the car. The day had been filled with revelations, each one adding a new layer of complexity to our investigation.

Meri, always quick with a quip, broke the silence that had settled in the car. "Well, that was quite the adventure," he remarked, a hint of amusement in his voice. "Breaking federal privacy laws and all. What's next on our detective to-do list?"

Thorn, ever the focused investigator, kept his eyes on the road as he responded. "We need to head back to the station, review what we've found, and plan our next steps."

And so, we made our way back to the sheriff's station, our minds busy piecing together the information we had gathered and contemplating the intricate puzzle that was slowly starting to take shape.

Upon our return to the sheriff's station, we found Jeremy waiting for us. He had been busy in our absence, continuing his investigation into At the Roots with the help of a forensic accountant, a buddy of his from college.

"Good, you're back," he greeted us, his expression serious. "I've been digging deeper into At the Roots' financials. It's not pretty."

He proceeded to lay out his findings. At the Roots had been using a complex network of shell companies to launder money and obscure their illicit activities. The scale of the operation was staggering, far beyond what one would expect from a small, local charity.

"But here's the kicker," Jeremy added, tapping a finger on a particular document. "Richard Blackwell's signature is on the incorporation documents for one of these shell companies."

The revelation hit us like a punch to the gut. It was the concrete link we had been searching for, tying Blackwell directly to the illegal activities of At the Roots.

Chapter Seventeen

With Jeremy's findings in hand, Thorn had the substantial evidence he needed to finally obtain a search warrant. He wasted no time in submitting the request, detailing the connections between Richard Blackwell, At the Roots, and the series of shell companies involved in money laundering.

The judge, faced with the compelling evidence, granted the warrant without hesitation. It was a significant breakthrough in our investigation. Now, we had the legal authority to search Richard Blackwell's mansion and his businesses, potentially uncovering more evidence of his involvement in the illicit activities.

"Finally," Thorn muttered, a sense of satisfaction in his voice as he held the approved warrant. "Now we can really dig into what Blackwell's been hiding."

***

The Blackwell mansion was an imposing sight as we approached. The sprawling estate was meticulously maintained, the manicured lawns and ornate architecture a stark contrast to the illicit activities we suspected were taking place within its walls.

Thorn was the first to step out of the car, the search warrant held firmly in his grasp. His expression was one of determination as he strode towards the front door, his steps echoing in the still morning air. The door was answered by a member of Richard's staff, a stern-faced butler whose eyes widened slightly at the sight of the law enforcement officers on the doorstep.

"Good morning," Thorn greeted, his tone professional and his demeanor calm. "We're here to execute a search warrant on this property. We need to come in."

The butler, though clearly taken aback, quickly regained his composure. "Mr. Blackwell is not here at the moment," he informed us, his voice steady despite the unexpected intrusion.

"That's not a problem," Thorn replied, handing him the warrant. "We'll proceed with the search in his absence."

With the formalities out of the way, Thorn and Jeremy began their search of the mansion. The other deputies, meanwhile, were tasked with keeping an eye on the staff, who were ushered outside onto the expansive lawn.

I, on the other hand, slipped in through a back door, my entrance unnoticed by the staff. Thorn had wanted me there during the search, and I was more than willing to lend my expertise.

The interior of the mansion was a labyrinth of grandeur, each room we passed more lavish than the last. The opulence was almost overwhelming. But it was not the visible extravagance that held our interest. Our true focus lay in the secrets hidden behind the mansion's ornate facade.

As we delved deeper into the mansion, we discovered a series of hidden rooms, their entrances cleverly concealed behind secret panels and disguised doors. It was as if we had stumbled into a different world, one that existed beneath the surface of Richard's ostentatious lifestyle.

These hidden rooms were filled with a staggering array of illegal magical artifacts and potions. Each item was meticulously arranged, their placement indicative of a person who understood their value and significance. The sight of such a vast collection of illicit items was an absolute revelation, providing a tangible link to the criminal activities we had been investigating.

The sheer scale of the operation was staggering. Each artifact, each potion… painted a picture of Richard's deep involvement in the illegal activities.

But the most damning evidence was yet to come. Amidst the artifacts and potions, we found documents - detailed records that linked Richard directly to the criminal organization's money-laundering scheme. As we sifted through the evidence, it became increasingly clear that Richard Blackwell was not just involved in the illegal activities - he was at the very heart of it.

Despite the trove of illicit items and the damning evidence of Richard's involvement in the criminal organization, we were unable to find concrete proof linking him to the attack on Isadora or the theft of the rare magical artifacts that had initially sparked our investigation.

We meticulously examined each artifact, each document, in the hope of finding a clue that would connect Richard to these specific crimes. But our search yielded no such evidence.

The absence of a direct link was frustrating, a gap in our understanding of the situation. It was clear that Richard was deeply involved in illegal activities, but the specific connection to Isadora's attack and the artifact thefts remained elusive.

***

As Thorn and I pulled up to Richard Blackwell's office building, I could feel a knot of anticipation tightening in my stomach. We had been through so much to get to this point, and now we were about to arrest one of the richest men in Coventry. I stayed in the car, watching as Thorn strode confidently into the building. He was a picture of professionalism, his demeanor calm and focused.

After what felt like an eternity, Thorn emerged from the building, flanked by Jeremy and a few other deputies. In their midst was Richard Blackwell, his hands cuffed in front of him. His face was a mask of shock and disbelief, his eyes darting around as if he was still trying to process what was happening.

They led him to Jeremy's cruiser, and I watched as they helped him into the back seat. The door closed with a finality that sent a shiver down my spine. Richard Blackwell, the wealthy businessman, the philanthropist, the respected member of our community, was under arrest.

The cruiser pulled away, heading back to the station where Richard would be booked and processed. Thorn returned to our car, his expression serious but satisfied. We had made a significant breakthrough in our investigation, but we both knew that this was far from over. Richard made bail easily and was release quickly. Too quickly, in my opinion…

Chapter Eighteen

The heat of the summer day had barely abated as
evening fell, leaving the air thick and sticky. Meri and
I were stationed in my car, parked strategically to
afford us a clear view of Blackwell's grand mansion,
its serene facade belying the secrets within.

Despite his recent arrest, Blackwell was out on bail,
but the shadow of suspicion still loomed large. Our
task was clear - to observe and report any unusual
activity that might further tie him to the ongoing
investigation.

As the sun set, the building stood silent and seemingly
deserted. We sat in the growing darkness, our senses
on high alert, our eyes scanning the area for any sign
of movement. The only sounds were the occasional
rustle of leaves and the distant hum of nocturnal
creatures, amplified in the quiet of the evening.

Suddenly, a figure emerged from the mansion.
Dressed in nondescript clothing, their face hidden by
a hoodie, strange attire given the heat, they moved
with a purpose that immediately drew our attention.
They quickly got into a parked car and drove off.

Meri and I exchanged a glance, a silent agreement
passing between us. This was suspicious and
potentially a significant lead. I started the car and we

followed at a safe distance as the hoodie-clad figure drove off toward the outskirts of town.

Meri and I found ourselves parked inconspicuously down the street from a quaint tea shop. The establishment, known as "Grace's Brews," was nestled amidst a row of charming, old-fashioned buildings. Its cheery sign and the warm, inviting glow emanating from its windows stood in stark contrast to the suspicious activity we were observing.

The tea shop was owned by Grace Sutherland, a woman who was something of a local legend. Known for her sweet nature, infectious laughter, and the best tea blends in town, Grace was a beloved figure in the community. Her tea shop was a popular spot, often filled with locals seeking a comforting cup of tea and a friendly chat. It was hard to reconcile this image with what we were witnessing.

As Meri and I sat in the car, the air thick with the heat of the summer evening, we watched a steady stream of individuals enter and exit the tea shop. These were not the usual clientele one would expect in such a place. They were a motley crew, their appearances ranging from the rough and rugged to the suspiciously nondescript. Their presence was jarring in the cozy, homey setting of the tea shop.

I glanced at Meri, his feline eyes narrowed in concentration as he observed the scene. The sight of these out-of-place individuals in Grace's Brews was a clear red flag. Something was going on, and we had inadvertently stumbled upon it.

"Let's check it out," I suggested, nodding towards the tea shop. Meri shot me a skeptical look, his nose wrinkling in distaste.

"A tea shop, Kinsley? Really? You know they don't serve bacon there, right?" he grumbled, his tone filled with playful annoyance.

I rolled my eyes, a small smile tugging at the corners of my mouth. "We're not going for the food, Meri. We're going to investigate."

With a resigned sigh, Meri hopped off the car seat and followed me towards the tea shop. As we stepped inside, the warm, comforting aroma of brewing tea and freshly baked pastries filled the air. The interior was charming, with cozy seating arrangements and vintage decor. A long counter displayed an array of tantalizing treats, and behind it, Grace Sutherland herself was serving customers with a warm smile.

We joined the queue at the counter, our eyes scanning the room. Among the regular townsfolk enjoying their tea and pastries, we spotted a couple of the suspicious characters we had seen earlier.

As we waited in line, Meri leaned in closer to me, his voice dropping to a whisper. "This place is too cute for my taste, Kinsley. And where's the bacon?" he grumbled, earning a soft chuckle from me. "Any place that doesn't serve bacon is a non-serious business in my opinion."

"Focus, Meri," I reminded him, my gaze fixed on the suspicious characters. "We're here to investigate, remember?"

As we moved closer to the counter, I noticed something peculiar. Grace seemed to be selling a lot of "marshmallow root." The herb was common enough, often used in teas for its soothing properties. But the frequency with which it was being requested was unusual.

As I observed Grace handling the herb, I felt a familiar magical signature. It was faint, almost imperceptible amidst the hustle and bustle of the shop, but it was unmistakable. It was the same magical signature I had detected from the rare herb involved in Isadora's attack.

When it was finally our turn to order, I decided to test my suspicion. "Could I get a bag of marshmallow root, please?" I asked, trying to keep my voice casual.

Grace, who had been all smiles and warmth with the previous customers, suddenly turned curt. "I'm afraid we're all out," she said, her tone dismissive.

I tried to press further, but she quickly moved on to the next customer, effectively ending our interaction. As I stepped away from the counter, I couldn't shake off the feeling that there was more to this quaint tea shop than met the eye.

Despite my best efforts to catch Grace's attention again, she seemed to have developed a sudden case of selective blindness. She moved around the counter, serving other customers, her gaze carefully avoiding mine. It was clear that she had no intention of engaging with me further.

Feeling a mix of frustration and suspicion, I eventually conceded defeat and made my way out of the shop, the bell above the door tinkling softly as I exited. The hot summer air hit me as I stepped outside.

Meri, however, lingered behind. He had a knack for blending into the background when he wanted to, his feline form easily overlooked amidst the hustle and bustle of the shop.

A few minutes later, he emerged from the shop, a smug grin on his face. "You were right," he said, hopping into the passenger seat of the car. "She sold more of that 'marshmallow root' after you left. And guess what? She was taking it from the same container she told you was empty."

Chapter Nineteen

I sat in my car, parked discreetly down the street from the tea shop. The summer heat still clung to the air, making the interior of the car stuffy despite the setting sun. My fingers drummed a nervous rhythm on the steering wheel as I dialed Thorn's number.

"Thorn, it's Kinsley," I said into the phone, my eyes flicking to the rearview mirror to keep an eye on the tea shop. "I think we've stumbled onto something."

I quickly relayed the events at the tea shop, from the suspicious characters to the supposed 'marshmallow root' that Grace was selling. I explained my suspicions about the herb and its potential connection to the illegal potion-making operation we'd been investigating.

There was a pause on the other end of the line, and then Thorn's voice came through, steady and reassuring. "All right, Kinsley. Stay put. I'm on my way."

I ended the call, sinking back into my seat as I continued to watch the tea shop.

As Thorn's cruiser pulled up behind my car, I could see the determined set of his jaw. Meri and I met him at the curb, quickly briefing him on our observations and suspicions.

"All right," Thorn said, his voice steady, "Let's do this."

We entered the tea shop, the soft jingle of the doorbell announcing our arrival. Grace looked up from behind the counter, her eyes widening in surprise as they darted between the three of us.

"Grace," Thorn began, his tone firm but not unkind. "We need to talk."

Her face paled noticeably, but she nodded, gesturing for us to follow her to a small table tucked away in the back of the shop. We took our seats, the air around us heavy with anticipation.

Thorn took a deep breath, steeling himself before he began. "Grace," he started, his voice steady and authoritative, "We've been conducting an investigation. We've noticed some... irregularities that we need to discuss with you."

Grace's eyes widened slightly, but she remained silent, giving Thorn the space to continue.

"We've observed some unusual activity here at your tea shop," Thorn continued, his gaze never leaving Grace's. "You have a lot of suspicious people coming and going. And they all seem to be purchasing the same thing - your marshmallow root."

At this, Grace's eyes flickered to me, a hint of apprehension creeping into her expression. I nodded, confirming Thorn's words. "I was in here earlier, Grace," I added, my voice softer than Thorn's but no less serious. "I asked to buy some of your marshmallow root, but you told me you were sold out. Yet, you continued to sell it after I left."

"And there's more," Thorn interjected, drawing Grace's attention back to him. "Kinsley here, she's got a knack for detecting magical signatures. And she picked up on something... off about your marshmallow root. It's got the same signature as a rare herb we've been investigating in relation to some... serious crimes."

As Thorn laid out our findings, Grace's face grew paler and paler. Her eyes darted between us, the realization of her situation slowly sinking in. By the time he finished, she was in tears, her hands trembling as they clutched at her apron.

"I... I didn't have a choice," she sobbed, her voice barely above a whisper. "The bills... my medication... I was desperate." Grace's shoulders slumped, and she let out a defeated sigh. "All right, you got me," she confessed, her voice tinged with resignation. "I've been making and selling the illegal potion."

Thorn raised an eyebrow, his expression a mix of curiosity and concern. "Why, Grace? Why would you get involved in something like this?"

Grace's gaze fell to the floor, and her voice trembled slightly as she answered, "I... I needed the money. I have medical expenses, and my retirement funds were running out. I thought if I could just supplement my income, I could make ends meet."

I could see a flicker of sympathy in Thorn's eyes, but he remained focused on the task at hand. "But why use the tea shop as a front? Why put your customers at risk?"

Grace let out a bitter laugh, a tinge of regret in her voice. "I thought no one would suspect a sweet old lady running a tea shop. And I didn't think it would cause any harm. I just wanted to make a living, that's all."

Thorn's tone softened slightly as he spoke, his voice laced with understanding. "Grace, I understand that times can be tough, but this is not the way to solve your problems. You've put yourself in serious legal trouble."

Grace nodded, tears welling up in her eyes. "I know... I know I made a terrible mistake. I'm sorry, truly."

Thorn glanced at me, silently conveying the need to handle the situation responsibly. "We'll have to take you into custody, Grace," he said, his voice firm but compassionate. "You'll need to face the consequences of your actions."

Grace nodded once again, her demeanor showing a mix of regret and acceptance. "I understand," she whispered, her voice filled with resignation. "I'll cooperate."

Thorn paused for a moment, his hand still on Grace's shoulder. "Grace, if you cooperate fully and provide us with valuable information, I promise we will do everything we can to consider leniency and potentially seek immunity for your cooperation."

Grace's eyes widened with a glimmer of hope. "You... you would do that?"

Thorn nodded solemnly. "We understand that there may be others involved, and if your cooperation helps us bring them down and dismantle the entire operation, it would be in everyone's best interest."

Grace took a deep breath, her voice filled with a mix of fear and determination. "All right, I'll tell you everything I know. This man who delivers the goods, he always wears a hoodie and uses some kind of spell to blur his face. He calls himself Deliverer, and he's the one who provides me with rare and expensive ingredients to create the potions."

Thorn exchanged a glance with me. "Do you have any idea who he might be? Any information that could help us identify him?"

Grace shook her head, frustration evident in her voice. "No, I'm sorry. He's always careful to hide his identity. I've never seen his face or heard his real name. He's just known as Deliverer."

Thorn sighed, realizing the challenge ahead. "Well, at least we have a lead to pursue."

"I never intended for things to turn out like this. I just wanted to survive."

***

Thorn and I found ourselves deep in discussion, our minds racing with possibilities as we contemplated the next course of action. The realization that Deliverer might be the elusive mastermind behind the criminal organization and the thefts of rare magical artifacts, and could have something to do with the attack on Isadora, had ignited a fierce determination within us.

Seated across from each other, the weight of the situation settled upon us. Papers and photographs lay scattered on the table, remnants of our investigation, while the air crackled with a mix of apprehension and unwavering resolve.

Thorn's piercing gaze met mine, concern etched in the furrows of his brow. "Kinsley, I understand your drive to confront Deliverer, but we must tread carefully. This is a dangerous path we're venturing into."

I nodded, acknowledging his caution. "I know, Thorn. It's a risk, but it's a risk we have to take. Deliverer holds the key to unraveling this entire criminal organization. We can't let him slip through our fingers."

Thorn leaned back in his chair, his voice tinged with worry. "Putting yourself in harm's way... it's a lot to ask, Kinsley. But I also recognize your capabilities. If we proceed, we need a solid plan. We can't afford any missteps."

"Thorn, I understand the risks involved, but I'm willing to take them. We can't let fear paralyze us."

Thorn sighed, his gaze softening as he regarded me. "I have complete faith in your abilities, Kinsley. We'll plan meticulously, ensuring we have the necessary support and backup. But promise me, promise me that you'll prioritize your safety above all else."

I met his concern with a determined smile. "Thorn, I promise. I'll be cautious, and I'll stay vigilant. We'll execute this operation flawlessly."

Meri interjected with a snarky remark, breaking the intensity of the moment. "Oh, here we go again, Kinsley, with your unwavering confidence and grand schemes. Have you forgotten the hilariously disastrous outcomes that often follow your overconfidence?"

I let out a sigh, knowing Meri had a point. "All right, Meri, no need to burst our bubble."

"Better to burst your bubble than stand back and watch you bust… well, everything around you."

"I'm thinking that maybe our family should go vegan," I said in response. "Better for our health and the environment…"

"Hey, sorry," Meri said. "No need to go crazy. I was just having a little fun."

"Sure."

"Whatever," he said and sashayed out of the room with his tail flicking from side to side.

Chapter Twenty

Grace's expression was cold and distant when I entered her tea shop. She was a petite woman, her usual warm demeanor replaced by a hardened exterior. She wasn't pleased to see me, but she had no choice. If she didn't cooperate, she'd be facing jail time for her role in the criminal organization.

We sat at a small table, the murmur of other patrons and the clinking of porcelain creating a subtle soundtrack to our tense conversation.

"Listen," Grace began, her voice barely above a whisper. "I can get you into a meeting with the members of the organization."

I raised an eyebrow at her. "How?"

She sighed, her fingers nervously tapping on the table. "You'll have to pose as a new buyer. They're always looking for new clients for their illegal potions."

The plan was risky, but it was the only shot we had at infiltrating their operation. I felt a knot of anxiety in my stomach, but I pushed it aside. This was not the time for fear.

"All right," I agreed, trying to keep my voice steady. "Let's do it."

With the plan set, I left the tea shop and made my way to the outskirts of town. The warehouse loomed in the distance, a hulking, ominous structure scarred by time and neglect. I took a deep breath, steeling myself for what was to come. I was about to walk into the lion's den, and I could only hope that I would walk out again. Grace's freedom, and my life, hung in the balance.

Stepping into the warehouse was like stepping into another world. The air was thick with dust and the smell of mold. A few members of the organization were already there, their faces partially hidden in the gloom. I swallowed hard, my heart pounding like a drum in my chest. I was playing a dangerous game, and I was acutely aware of the stakes.

"I'm interested in acquiring a direct source for some of Grace's 'marshmallow root,'" I began, trying to keep my voice steady. The 'marshmallow root' was a code name, a euphemism for one of the illegal ingredients Grace was known to deal in. I continued, listing off a few other names of illegal plants and herbs that sprang to mind. These were substances so potent, so perilous, that even Lilith, the notorious potion master, would think twice before handling them.

One of the members, a man built like a brick wall with a jagged scar marring his cheek, grunted in response. He named a price for some of the items I'd asked for, his gravelly voice echoing in the vast space of the warehouse. "I'll have to look into the rest," he said, his gaze never wavering from mine. His eyes were cold, calculating, and I had to fight the urge to look away.

Just as I was beginning to think that I might pull this off, that the plan might actually work, everything started to unravel. One of the members, a woman with a wiry frame and eyes that missed nothing, squinted at me. "Hold on," she said, her voice slicing through the silence like a knife. "You were at the tea shop earlier, snooping around."

My heart lurched in my chest. I had been careful, or so I thought, but it seemed I hadn't been careful enough. Before I could formulate a response, another member, a tall man with a snake tattoo winding up his arm, chimed in. "And you're the sheriff's wife," he said, a slow, knowing smile spreading across his face.

The warehouse fell silent, the only sound the distant drip of water from a leaky pipe. I could feel the atmosphere shift, the danger level escalating exponentially. The plan had gone horribly wrong, and I was standing in a room full of criminals who knew exactly who I was. I was no longer a potential buyer; I was a threat, and I had no idea what they planned to do about it.

The moment the man's words echoed in the cavernous warehouse, the room was thrown into a whirlwind of action. The members of the organization lunged at me, their faces twisted into snarls of rage and betrayal. I reacted on pure instinct, my magic surging to life in my hands. With a swift motion, I sent a wave of raw energy towards the nearest attacker. He was thrown backwards, his body slamming into a stack of crates with a loud crash. But there were too many of them. Despite my magic, I was vastly outnumbered, and I could feel the tide of the battle turning against me.

Just as I was bracing myself for the onslaught, the warehouse doors were thrown open with a deafening bang. Thorn, the town's sheriff, stormed into the room. His face was set in a grim mask of determination, his hand gripping his service pistol tightly. He pointed his gun at the advancing members, a clear warning. But they didn't stop.

Thorn fired, the sharp report of his gun echoing in the warehouse. But the members used magic to deflect the bullets, their faces twisted in malicious glee. Seeing his gun was ineffective, Thorn holstered it and charged into the fray, his fists flying.

Meri darted into the room alongside him. Despite his size, Meri was not to be underestimated. His movements were swift and precise, a blur of fur and claws as he weaved between the legs of the attackers.

His sharp claws left deep scratches on exposed skin, and his magic created a distraction, giving Thorn and me the openings we needed to fight back.

Together, we pushed back against the members of the organization. Thorn's brute strength, my magic, and Meri's agility and cunning began to shift the balance of the fight. One by one, the members were apprehended, their threats neutralized. But not all of them.

In the midst of the chaos, Deliverer, the elusive and cunning leader of the organization, managed to slip away. I caught a fleeting glimpse of him disappearing into the shadows, his mocking laughter echoing hauntingly in the cavernous space of the warehouse. He had escaped our grasp.

The moment we saw Deliverer's modest sedan pulling away from the warehouse, we knew we had to act fast. He was making his escape, heading away from Coventry and into the maze of country roads that stretched out into the darkness. Thorn, Meri, and I didn't hesitate. We scrambled into Thorn's cruiser, the engine roaring to life under Thorn's experienced hand.

Thorn was more than competent at the wheel. He was an experienced driver, his years as sheriff evident in the way he expertly navigated the cruiser. The tires squealed as he gunned the engine, the cruiser lurching forward in hot pursuit of Deliverer's sedan.

The chase was on. The sedan's taillights glowed like twin beacons in the darkness, weaving and bobbing as Deliverer tried to lose us on the winding country roads. But Thorn was relentless. He kept the cruiser right on the sedan's tail, the powerful headlights illuminating the back of the fleeing vehicle.

With a sudden burst of speed, Thorn pulled the cruiser up alongside Deliverer's car. He was close, so close I could see the silhouette of Deliverer hunched over the wheel. Thorn didn't hesitate. He jerked the cruiser to the side, executing a perfect pit maneuver. Deliverer's car spun out, the tires screeching in protest as it skidded to a halt in a cloud of dust on the side of the road.

We jumped out of the cruiser. Thorn approached the sedan, his gun drawn and ready. I followed, my magic humming in my veins, ready to be unleashed at a moment's notice. Meri stayed close to my side, his fur bristling and his eyes glowing in the darkness.

Thorn yanked open the driver's door, his gun pointed at the figure hunched in the seat. "Get out," he ordered, his voice echoing in the still night air.

Slowly, Deliverer complied. He stepped out of the car, his hands raised in surrender. He was wearing a hoodie, the hood pulled up to obscure his face. With a swift motion, Thorn reached out, pulling back the hood.

The face that was revealed left us in shock. It was Miles Taylor. In case you don't remember, that's the mayor of Coventry. His face was pale in the moonlight, his eyes wide with fear. He was the Deliverer, the leader of the criminal organization we had been trying to take down. We had him now, and we weren't going to let him slip away again.

Thorn moved swiftly, cuffing Miles' hands behind his back. "Miles Taylor, you're under arrest," he declared, his voice stern. But Miles didn't seem fazed. Instead, he shook his head, a bitter laugh escaping his lips.

"You've got it all wrong," he said, his voice steady despite his predicament. "I'm not the ringleader."

Thorn and I exchanged a glance. This was unexpected. Miles continued, his words tumbling out in a rush.

"I got involved because I needed the money," he confessed. "I wanted to fund my campaign, maintain my lifestyle. But I'm not in charge. I'm just a pawn in this game."

He paused, taking a deep breath before dropping the bombshell. "Richard Blackwell is my boss. He's the one pulling the strings. He's the one with the big plans."

Chapter Twenty-One

As Thorn was finishing up with Miles, the distant rumble of an approaching vehicle echoed through the quiet country road. Moments later, the headlights of another cruiser cut through the darkness, coming to a halt beside us. Jeremy stepped out of the vehicle. His eyes widened in surprise as he took in the sight of the apprehended mayor, but he quickly composed himself, professionalism taking over.

Without a word, Jeremy moved to take Miles into custody, his movements efficient and practiced. He loaded Miles into the back of his cruiser, his face stern as he read him his rights. With Miles now in the hands of the law, Thorn turned his attention to the new threat that had just been revealed - Richard Blackwell.

"I'm going to Richard's home," Thorn announced, his voice grim with determination. He turned to me, his eyes filled with a mix of concern and pleading. "Kinsley, I need you to stay back. It's too dangerous."

But I was already shaking my head, my resolve firm. "I'm coming with you," I declared, meeting his gaze without flinching. "Meri and I, we're in this together. And it's more dangerous for you than it is for us. You need us on this."

Thorn sighed, a resigned look crossing his face. He knew better than to argue with me when I had made up my mind. "All right," he conceded, his voice heavy. "But stay close. We don't know what we're walking into."

"You should stay close to me," I quipped.

"Maybe not her," Meri groused. "She might blow you up or summon a demon to harvest your soul… anyway, you guys should stay close to me."

"Whatever," Thorn said, and I laughed.

Meri just harrumphed and swished his tail.

With that, we climbed back into Thorn's cruiser, the engine roaring to life as we set off into the night. The taillights of Jeremy's cruiser faded into the distance as we headed towards Richard's home, the apprehended mayor now a part of our rearview mirror. We had managed to capture Miles, but the real threat, it seemed, was still at large. Richard Blackwell was out there, and we were heading straight for him.

We arrived at Richard's mansion, and Thorn led the way, his hand resting on the butt of his gun. I followed closely behind, my magic humming in my veins, a force ready to be unleashed at a moment's notice. Meri was at my side, his fur bristling, his eyes glowing with a fierce intensity in the darkness.

Thorn knocked on the door, the sound echoing through the silent night. After a moment, the door creaked open, and Richard stood in the entrance. It was strange that he answered the door himself, but his staff must have been off for the night. His face registered surprise as he saw us, but he quickly composed himself and stepped aside, allowing us to enter the grand foyer of his home.

Once inside the grand foyer of Richard's home, Thorn wasted no time. "Mayor Taylor gave you up, Richard," he announced, his voice echoing in the high-ceilinged room. Richard's face flickered with surprise, but he quickly masked it with a smirk.

"Is that so?" he replied, his voice dripping with feigned innocence. His gaze shifted to a small table nearby, where a vial sat, its contents shimmering ominously under the dim light of the chandelier above.

Without breaking eye contact, Richard reached for the vial. His fingers wrapped around it, lifting it off the table with a deliberate slowness. He uncorked it and downed its contents in one swift motion. It was the illicit potion, the same one that had been causing so much trouble in Coventry.

We watched in trepidation as Richard's body convulsed, his back arching as the potion took effect. His eyes began to glow with a newfound power, the whites replaced by a vibrant, almost unnatural color. His smirk widened, transforming into a full-blown grin as he reveled in the surge of power coursing through his veins.

The transformation was terrifying to witness. The once composed and sophisticated Richard was now a formidable, powered-up version of himself. His magic, already potent, was now amplified by the potion.

As soon as Richard's transformation was complete, the room descended into chaos. Richard, now supercharged by the potion, was a formidable adversary. His movements were swift and precise, his magic potent and destructive. He moved with a predator's grace, his eyes glowing with malicious intent.

Meri was the first to react. He darted forward, his small form a blur of fur and claws. He weaved around Richard, his claws slashing through the air, leaving deep scratches on Richard's exposed skin. But Richard was quick, his enhanced reflexes allowing him to dodge most of Meri's attacks. Undeterred, Meri unleashed his own magic, a series of quick, sharp bursts of energy that kept Richard on his toes.

I was right behind Meri, my magic at the ready. I unleashed wave after wave of raw energy, each one crashing against Richard's defenses. But Richard was strong, his magic deflecting most of my attacks. It was clear that subduing him was going to take everything we had.

Thorn was not idle during this. He may not have had magic, but he had years of experience and a strength that was all his own. He moved in, his fists flying, landing punch after punch on Richard. But Richard was quick, his enhanced reflexes allowing him to dodge most of Thorn's attacks.

Despite the odds, we didn't back down. Meri and I continued our magical assault, while Thorn used his strength and skill to keep Richard off balance. All the while, Thorn kept his warded handcuffs at the ready, waiting for the perfect moment to subdue Richard. The fight was brutal and exhausting, but we kept going.

Finally, I managed to cast a spell that kept Richard compliant, his movements becoming sluggish and uncoordinated. Thorn seized the opportunity, moving in to cuff Richard. The warded handcuffs glowed as they locked around Richard's wrists, their magic neutralizing his.

With Richard subdued, we loaded him into the cruiser, the journey back to the jailhouse tense and silent. As we arrived, we were surprised to find Lilith waiting for us. She was a formidable figure, her presence commanding the room. Her eyes were cold, her expression unreadable.

She gestured towards the jail with a dismissive wave of her hand. "Put him in a cell," she instructed Thorn, her voice devoid of any emotion. "And then leave him to me. I'll question him and ultimately deal with him."

Thorn nodded, leading Richard to a cell. As the cell door closed behind Richard with a resounding clang... I knew he was most likely done for...

***

It was a tranquil day that Thorn and I found ourselves on the road, heading to pick up Laney and Hekate from their magical summer camp. The camp, which had been their home for several fun-filled weeks, had finally come to an end.

Upon our arrival at the camp, we were greeted by the sight of our daughters. Laney and Hekate came bounding towards us, their faces glowing with the excitement of seeing us after their time away. Their eyes sparkled with joy, their smiles wide and genuine. Laney had Bonkers trailing behind her. His tail swished in contentment, clearly happy to be reunited with Meri. Their joy was infectious, and I couldn't help but smile at their enthusiasm. Meri was not nearly as pleased.

Once we were all settled in the car, with Bonkers comfortably curled up in Laney's lap, the journey home began. The car ride was filled with their excited chatter, their voices filling the vehicle with a lively energy. It was during this journey that Hekate turned to us, her eyes wide with curiosity. "Did we miss anything while we were gone?" she asked, her voice filled with anticipation.

"No, it was a quiet few weeks," I reassured them, offering a comforting smile. I decided it was best to keep them in the dark about the recent events, not wanting to worry them with the complexities of our adult world.

As we continued our drive back, I noticed Meri whispering with the girls in the backseat. I couldn't hear what they were saying, but the intrigued looks on my daughters' faces told me they were discussing something interesting. It seemed Meri was sharing some secrets of his own.

Was he telling them about the most recent murder and investigation? It seemed so.

Observing them, I felt a complex swirl of emotions. There was pride, certainly, as their curiosity and burgeoning interest in investigation mirrored my own passions. It was heartening to see them take after me in this way, their inquisitive minds eager to uncover the mysteries of the world around them.

Yet, there was also a thread of worry woven into my pride. For the time being, I resolved to let them bask in the innocence of their childhood.

For as long as the world... and Meri... would let me.

***

Later that night, with the girls safely tucked into bed, I found myself gazing out of the window. The street outside was bathed in the soft glow of the moonlight. It was then that I noticed her - the woman with sapphire hair. She was standing across the street, her gaze fixed on our house. Her striking hair glowed under the moonlight, making her an ethereal figure in the quiet night.

A decision made, I stepped outside onto the front porch. The cool night air brushed against my skin as I moved closer to the edge, my eyes never leaving the woman. We stared at each other for a full minute, the silence between us filled with unspoken words and questions.

Finally, I broke the silence. "Would you like to come over for a cup of coffee?" I called out, my voice echoing in the quiet street. She studied me for a few more moments, her eyes reflecting the moonlight. Then, she called back, her voice carrying across the distance between us, "Maybe another time."

With that, she turned and walked off into the night, her sapphire hair catching the moonlight as she disappeared from view. I watched her until she was out of sight, a sense of anticipation settling in my heart. Our paths had crossed once again, and I had a feeling it wouldn't be the last time.

Thank you for reading!

Made in United States
North Haven, CT
30 July 2023

39717326R00134